One of the Survivors

Susan Shaw

Margaret K. McElderry Books

NEW YORK LONDON TORONTO SYDNEY

If you purchased this book without a cover, you should be aware that this book is stolen property. It was reported as "unsold and destroyed" to the publisher, and neither the author nor the publisher has received any payment for this "stripped book."

MARGARET K. McELDERRY BOOKS

An imprint of Simon & Schuster Children's Publishing Division

1230 Avenue of the Americas, New York, New York 10020

This book is a work of fiction. Any references to historical events, real people, or real locales are used fictitiously. Other names, characters, places, and incidents are products of the author's imagination, and any resemblance to actual events or locales or persons, living or dead, is entirely coincidental.

Copyright © 2009 by Susan Shaw

All rights reserved, including the right of reproduction in whole or in part in any form.

MARGARET K. McELDERRY BOOKS is a trademark of Simon & Schuster, Inc.

For information about special discounts for bulk purchases, please contact Simon & Schuster Special Sales at 1-866-506-1949 or business@simonandschuster.com.

The Simon & Schuster Speakers Bureau can bring authors to your live event. For more information or to book an event, contact the Simon & Schuster Speakers Bureau at 1-866-248-3049 or visit our website at www.simonspeakers.com.

Also available in a Margaret K. McElderry Books hardcover edition.

Book design by Mike Rosamilia

The text for this book is set in Edlund and Trade Gothic Light.

Manufactured in the United States of America

0311 OFF

First Margaret K. McElderry Books paperback edition April 2011

10 9 8 7 6 5 4 3 2 1

The Library of Congress has cataloged the hardcover edition as follows:

Shaw, Susan, 1951–

One of the survivors / Susan Shaw.

p. cm.

Summary: When his classmates die in a school fire, fourteen-year-old Joey is haunted by their deaths and struggles to survive amidst suspicion and anger from the town.

ISBN 978-1-4169-6129-1 (hc)

ISBN 978-1-4169-6389-9 (pbk)

ISBN 978-1-4169-9656-9 (eBook)

[1. Grief—Fiction. 2. Death—Fiction. 3. Anger—Fiction. 4. Guilt—Fiction. 5. Fires—Fiction. 6. Schools—Fiction.]

I. Title. PZ7.S534343On 2009

[Fic]—dc22

2008035965

To Mom

Acknowledgments

Many thanks to my editor, Lisa Cheng, for her wonderful contributions to this work, and to my agent, Alyssa Eisner Henkin, for bringing it to her attention. Also big thank-yous to John, Warren, Terry, and Martha for all their critiques and encouragement along the way, and also thanks to the whole Wetherill-Shaw clan for their great belief in me. Hugs and kisses all around!

1.

FIRE!

Columns of fire, jets of fire, spirals of fire! Hot and orange and sparking all around me.

"Come on, Joey," Preston said with Maureen's scared voice. "Come *on*." He gave me a last backward glance through the veils of smoke. He walked a few more steps, and then I couldn't see him anymore.

"Preston!" I tried to go after him, but something had me by the belt. *"Preston!"*

I couldn't move forward, I couldn't move backward, and Preston—I had to save Preston.

A door. I saw a door. I banged on it with my fists, but it wouldn't open. "Mom!" I shouted, but she didn't answer. "Mom! Mo-*o*-om!"

Orange. Orange all around. Orange and black and soot,

and where was Preston? Where was Preston, and where was Pete? Where was Pete and where was Cheryl and where was Jamaal and Donnie and and and—

Mr. Bednarik showed up, a black shadow against the orange. He had a crowbar, and we were going to get in after all. Everything would be fine.

But the crowbar melted when it touched the door. The door melted too, and flowed around my feet like hot lava. All I could see behind where it had been was orange and black and black and orange, all roaring and jumping and snapping sparks.

Mr. Bednarik pulled me away, but I fought him. Why wouldn't he let me go? I knew we could still save them. I knew we could put on our fireproof suits and still save them. The fireproof suits—they were just over there, just out of sight, but I couldn't get at them with Mr. Bednarik pulling on me like that. Shaking me.

"Wake up, Joey." Shaking me. "Wake up." Shaking—

I opened my eyes. Dad was bent over me, his hair all spiky from his pillow, and I was sweating on the kitchen floor. Preston's green eyes looked down at me from a windowsill.

Home.

No fire.

Safe.

Dad stopped shaking me, and I sat up. "You were having a bad dream," he said. "You were shouting."

"I couldn't open the door," I mumbled. "I tried."

"I know, Joey. Get up. Get up and get a drink of water. Get rid of the dream."

As if I could.

But I got a drink of water, and then Dad and I went outside to stand together in the backyard. It was probably quiet out there, but I still felt the rage of the fire.

"There's the Big Dipper." Dad's voice cut through the flames, and they got farther away, became less bright. "See it?" He slapped at a mosquito.

I looked for it. "No, but I believe you."

He put his arm around my shoulders so our temples almost met and our eyes were on the same level. The flames moved off some more, and I felt the cool of the night. Dad pointed with his free hand.

"See it?" He slapped at another mosquito.

While I stared, the random stars came together, and I saw it. The Big Dipper. Right. There. Anyone could see it.

After a few more minutes of constellation searching, the bugs were really getting to Dad. He swatted and swatted.

"Okay now?" he asked. *Swat! Swat!* We climbed the steps to the porch. *Swat!* "Do you think you can sleep?"

"I'll be fine," I said. "It was just a dream."

We went back inside, and I returned to the sleeping bag by the kitchen's sliding glass door. Preston was still stretched out on the windowsill, his eyes reflecting the light Dad hadn't turned off in the dining room yet.

"Meowrr?" he asked.

"All okay, Preston," I answered. I punched up my pillow before lying down on it. "All okay." Lying down on it and feeling that hole I lived in. The gray hole that never went away. Not all okay.

2.

I couldn't stand it inside, and I couldn't go outside, not with the chanters and the trash throwers and the whoever-elses out there. So I went to stay with Ruby-ruby and her second husband, Albert, in Beverly, New Jersey.

"Once the fence is up," Dad promised me, "you can come home and be outside all you want."

Ruby-ruby. Nobody else's grandmother is called Ruby-ruby, and I don't know why mine is, but Pete Vitti used to call his grandmother Bomber. That was how he had twisted "Grandmom" out of his mouth when he was little, and she got stuck with that. People still call her that, including me, even if Pete can't.

In Beverly, Ruby-ruby gave me a bedroom with a bay window that tunneled the wind from the Delaware River straight on through to the hall door all day long.

I hoped the Delaware's air would blow the gray hole away from me. It didn't happen, but Beverly was still better than home right then, and it was good in that room, almost as good as being outside. I could manage to lie down and sleep there.

Ruby-ruby let me sleep late in the mornings and walk along the river in the afternoons or after dinner. The Delaware is pretty wide along Beverly, but you can make out Pennsylvania from there all right. Not that wide. I looked over during my walks and thought, *Dad and Preston are over there. Maureen's over there.*

Sometimes Ruby-ruby came with me, and sometimes we played Scrabble in her dining room with the old dolls from her childhood sitting in high chairs around the table like little kids waiting for lunch. Only quiet. Then we'd put the game away, and she'd make me tomato soup with crackers. Those round crackers that go so good with peanut butter. While the old dolls watched. Mariel. Mariel was her favorite.

"You can do that with dolls," said Ruby-ruby one of those days. "Have favorites. Just don't do it with real children."

I nodded, swallowing that hot soup.

She poured me some more before I asked for it. "Put some meat on those bones," she said.

"You're treating me like I'm an invalid," I said to her.

"You are an invalid, Joey," she said. "Eat. Get your strength."

Well, I didn't get that about being an invalid. I walked and talked, didn't I?

Just didn't think so good.

Once, after dinner, I walked along the Delaware and stopped to watch a boat go by. Then I sort of got stuck there watching the water where the boat had been and feeling the breeze and watching the dot where the boat had been and feeling the breeze and watching the dot until it was getting dark and the boat was probably halfway to Spain or someplace, and there was Albert.

"What are you doing, Joey?" he asked.

I blinked at him. That was when I saw how dark the day had become.

Albert took my arm, and I left the riverbank with him. Ruby-ruby had popcorn and soda waiting for us when we got back, to eat and drink while we watched the Phillies on TV. Once in a while somebody scored or made a great catch, and Albert shouted and Ruby-ruby yelled, "'Ray!" and I woke up kind of and saw the replay. I think it was the Phillies, but Ruby-ruby and Albert follow the Braves, too. It could have been the Braves.

The next afternoon I was sitting on Ruby-ruby's front porch taking knots out of yarn while she knitted something for a baby about to be born up the street.

"Have you ever read *Hamlet*?" Ruby-ruby asked.

"*Hamlet*? You mean Shakespeare?"

Ruby-ruby nodded. "That's the one."

"No. We read *A Midsummer Night's Dream* in eighth grade. We're supposed to read *King Lear* next year."

"Well, read *Hamlet* also."

"Why?"

Ruby-ruby paused in her knitting and squinted at me. "I'll tell you," she said. "Then you read it. You'll see what I mean."

I pulled a knot apart. "Okay." Started on another.

"Hamlet is a prince," said Ruby-ruby. "His mother's name is Gertrude, and his father's name was Hamlet too."

"He passed that name on?" I asked. "Didn't he like his kid?"

Ruby-ruby laughed. "Maybe not. I never thought of it that way." She laughed again. "That could bring a whole new interpretation to the play. Maybe that was really what was wrong with Hamlet, having to inherit that name. Anyway, King Hamlet gets killed, the king's brother Claudius marries Gertrude, and then Claudius gets to be king."

Then she went on to tell me how Hamlet knew Claudius was the murderer because he ended up as Gertrude's husband.

"What was the proof?" I asked.

"Oh, Hamlet just knew it," said Ruby-ruby. "Claudius became her husband, so that meant he was the murderer."

"What?" I struggled with a knot. "What about the facts?"

Ruby-ruby shrugged. "People don't always care about facts," she said. "Like Hamlet, they just know what they want to believe."

I stopped with the knot and looked straight at her. "Why are you telling me this?"

"I thought you might recognize some people from school in this play," she said. "Read it. That'll give you a better idea."

Then Ruby-ruby got up to start the pork chops and left me there on the porch working out purple knots and watching the cars go by. Watching the cars go by and working out purple knots. Mostly watching the cars go by. Seven blue, three convertibles—two white and a yellow—and an orange hatchback. A red motorcycle that revved real loud, and a kid on a bike with a black backpack over his shoulders. The bike was blue. So the blues won.

After a while Ruby-ruby called me in to set the table for dinner, and I left the purple knots on my porch chair. Maybe they're still there. Or maybe Ruby-ruby got Albert to ease out the rest of the knots and that purple yarn is now a vest or a hat that someone will wear during a snowball fight next winter. Purple against white.

I don't know because Dad came for me the next day. Before we left, Ruby-ruby gave us a basket of food to take home.

"I know your dad doesn't much like cooking," she said to me with a wink.

At home we found a copy of *Hamlet* tucked under the napkins.

The fence was up, and I was home again eating apples on the back porch. Eating apples and sleeping outside and feeling the breeze and eating apples and counting the cars driven by that I saw through the fence. Sometimes I counted just the blue ones, sometimes just the red ones, but mostly there weren't any to count because we lived on a small street and nobody much came by.

But there were always some.

3.

"Throw it! Throw it, Joey!"

I lateraled the football to Pete. He caught it and then threw it to Donnie, who threw it back to me. Then I threw it again to Pete, only I didn't really, just faked it, and while the other kids chased Pete, I . . .

Another time, our class took a field trip to the Franklin Institute. The best thing we saw was the giant heart you could walk through. *Thump!* Thump-*thump!* *Thump!* Thump-*thump!*

On the bus afterward, Pete and I teased some of the girls, going, *"Thump!* Thump-*thump!"* right in their ears.

They got kind of mad, but we kept doing it.

"Didn't you learn anything else?" Teresa shouted over our thumps.

"Thump! Thump-*thump!"*

"What about the planetarium?"

"*Thump!* Thump-*thump!*"

"What about the train exhibit?"

"*Thump!* Thump-*thump!*"

Teresa pulled a paper bag down over her head so all we could see was a little bit of brown hair sticking out the bottom. Pete and I laughed so hard at that, we could hardly get out any more *thumps!*

The next day, I brought in a bunch of plastic heart boxes, spring-loaded with little frogs that jumped out at you when they opened. Mom had brought them home from her store after Valentine's Day, but she let me take them, and Pete and I put them on everybody's desk in homeroom, going, *"Croak! Croak-croak! Croak! Croak-croak!"*

No matter what anybody said, we went, *"Croak! Croak-croak!"*

It cracked everybody up, even Ms. deWitt, and then all the other kids were going *Croak!* with us and throwing the plastic hearts back and forth or springing the frogs at one another. Ms. deWitt started not to like it so much when we wouldn't shut up for the announcements. That's when Pete and I went into the monkey itch, making loud monkey noises. *Wa-ha-hahahahaa!* Itch, itch. *Wa-ha-hahahahaa!* Itch, itch. That shut up the others, and then . . .

Well, there was the time I brought a pinwheel to school for each kid. Whenever we raised our hands, up came the pinwheels. Ms. Barrett, the French teacher, got a little too bugged, so we put them away before she got as far as taking them from us. I took mine out again in Mr. Trama's science class and waved it when he asked his first question, and then everybody did, some of them going *Croak!* Croak-*croak!* because they remembered the plastic hearts thing. We waved the pinwheels back and forth like we were in some kind of air chorus, except for the *croaks* that went off like little explosions around the room.

"Ha-ha-ha!" That was Mr. Trama. "Ha-ha-ha!"

Then he did a whole lesson on wind. That was the day we were supposed to dissect frogs, too.

We never did. Some kids minded, but three girls thanked me later for getting us out of that.

"I'd have thrown up, for sure," said Priscilla.

"Me too," said Cheryl.

"Me too," said Simone.

Then I was glad we didn't dissect the frogs. I figured twelve-year-olds didn't really *have* to see frog guts, and missing out on the throwing up part was a definite plus. Not seeing frog guts in seventh grade couldn't wreck your life or anything.

I still have my pinwheel from that day. Somewhere. Mom had gotten them at her store. They were a promotion, and they all said THINK GREEN!

And until May some of the kids still brought up that day.

"You don't pull jokes like that anymore," said Melanie once last winter.

That was true. Not since two Christmases ago.

"You should do that again with piñatas," Melanie had added. "My mother has a bunch of little ones. And squeaky toys. We could do it together."

I thought about it, but . . . what was funny?

"You do it," I told her, but she never did.

What I remember about all those days is how hard everybody laughed. So hard, Donnie fell off his chair. So hard, Priscilla had to go to the girls' room. So hard, Myrna cried. So hard, so hard, so h . . .

Did we really laugh that hard?

It doesn't feel real now.

What's funny?

4.

June 20th

Dad came out and dropped this notebook into my lap. "Write something," he said before going back inside.

Write something? *Huh!* There isn't anything worth writing about in the entire history of mankind. I hurled the notebook across the yard. Hurled it *hard*!

But it just sat there, its red cover shining in the sun like it was warm and at peace with being thrown out there, and it wouldn't shut up or fade or melt into the grass for anything.

I left the porch to throw it farther, maybe to get it behind one of the trees or, even better, over the fence and into the woods and just away. I didn't want to see it or think about it. I just wanted to sit on the porch steps and be left alone. But when I picked it up, I managed to grab it only by the red part, and it flipped open.

Mr. Trama.

That sketch is the only thing that's in this notebook. I guess I didn't take any notes that year. No, I probably lost this and got another one. And now here it is, resurfacing from under my old Rollerblades or something.

The sketch isn't too bad. It looks like Mr. Trama. I kind of remember drawing it.

So I wrote about that. *Okay, Dad? I did what you wanted. I wrote something.*

Seventeen lines. Only seventeen million to go. All these empty pages.

I always hated it when Miss Ferdinand told us to write themes or stories in English class. All the other kids would be writing, and I'd be looking at them write, wondering how they knew anything to put down. My mind would be a big silver blank. Like a movie screen before the movie starts.

"Get writing," Miss Ferdinand would say to me. "I'm grading this."

Then I'd write about getting told to write something and how it was going to be graded, so I better write it. The third time I did that, Miss Ferdinand asked me, "Do you really have nothing to say? Is nothing on your mind?"

And here's what I thought. *Sure, maybe I have something on my mind, but maybe I don't want to tell you. How is what's in my head your business? Shouldn't our thoughts be private?*

But I only smiled and said, "I just go blank." Because I'm not a troublemaker. Mom would call me a people-pleaser if she could see me now, and I guess that's what I am. I do my homework on time and don't make trouble for substitute teachers. No more practical jokes. Follow the rules and do what I'm told.

Except for the cigarettes. Dad wouldn't like it if he knew about the cigarettes. But I don't smoke them anymore. Not since May.

What should I write about?

How about this: I'm a fourteen-year-old boy named Joseph Edward Campbell. I'm five foot eight, one hundred twenty-five pounds. A skinny white kid with freckles and crazed black hair.

I'll be fifteen in September. September fifteenth.

Exactly a year after that, I'm quitting school. On my sixteenth birthday. Pennsylvania state law says I can do that. So I guess I'll *start* my junior year. Start it and quit right away. Maybe I'll just stop showing up at school before I make it all the way to sixteen. What could anyone do to me? But that's more than a year away. And where it is that I'm going to stop showing up, I don't know.

Well, I've got this pen in my hand, and I've written stuff, but that's it. What's to write about? I see only a blank in my brain. A white blank that's almost silver. Blank and shiny like aluminum foil. Blank, blank, blank. No thoughts, no brains.

Nothing.

The first thing I did in this notebook today wasn't writing. It was me pushing real hard through the pages in the back with the ballpoint pen, cutting through the layers of paper, making the pages stick together. But it's only paper in a spiral-bound notebook, and what does cutting it do? It doesn't fix anything, even after you bounce the notebook off the side of the house as hard as you can. It just lies there on the porch floor. Throwing it is just as useful as slamming doors.

Afterward, you have what you had before, except for the endless echo of the *slam* inside your ear with no one saying *Sorry* or making things better. Making things better. How could anybody make things better?

24 Dead, 2 Survivors. How can you fix that?

TELL ME HOW!

5.

the

June 21ˢᵗ

Journals aren't like other kinds of books. They don't have to be about anything. You don't have to follow any rules like making sense or capitalizing the first word in a sentence or using commas or topic sentences. Or you can write only topic sentences.

Like

Train engines require regular maintenance.
Brushing teeth prevents tooth decay.
There are three different kinds of rock.

But none of that matters.

It doesn't matter because you write it but you don't read it. It doesn't have to be right. It doesn't have to be wrong. It doesn't have to be anything.

I'm not going to read it. No one's going to read it. The only thing happening here is me writing with this pen. Only me writing in a red notebook on this porch with the gray wooden floor while the cat watches. There is nobody else that will come on this porch. Except Dad once in a while with some apples or some tangerines or grapes, but he won't read this. Not without my permission. And he won't stay because the mosquitoes can smell him from a mile away.

I need to think of blues and greens and oranges—not oranges. Except the fruit. I can think about the orange you eat.

Sweet juicy oranges and grapefruits and lemons and tangerines and clementines that are so little and sweet it's like eating candy.

Sometimes Dad buys clementines and leaves them out on the kitchen counter still in the wooden box they come in. Every time you walk through the room, you take one or two and eat them while you're on your way somewhere. You get as far as your bike, and you've got a handful of clementine peels and no place to put them but your pockets. So then Dad says you have to do your own wash after twice the clementine peels wind up in the dryer. And he's bugged at you.

Why am I writing about myself like I'm somebody else? I'm the one who stuffed clementine peels into my jeans pockets and forgot about them. But they didn't stay there forever the way the sandwiches and the gym socks did in my school locker.

One of the Survivors

Boy, peanut butter and jelly sandwiches do not smell good after a while! And the gym socks. They sure stank.

Why didn't I ever bring the gym socks home? But they were hard and crusty. Useless. Why would I bring them home? I should have thrown them out, but I put them in my locker, and that's where they stayed. I never felt like taking the extra minute to throw them into the trash can that was just down the hall. Crusty. I didn't want to touch them. The sandwiches had crusts too, but a different kind of crust. Last time I looked, they were a sort of bluish green. Ugh. I never looked again.

So I left all that in there, pushed to the back so I couldn't see them, but the smell still hit me in the face every time I opened the door. I guess the stink wasn't bad enough because I didn't do anything about it. I would have thrown the junk away when I cleaned out everything at the end of the school year.

In middle school our homeroom teachers would make us clean out our lockers once in a while. At the high school, nobody cares. Cared.

What's a moldy sandwich in a burned-out building?

6.

June 23rd

Today I'm writing about autumn leaves.

Leaves. What can anyone write about leaves? In the fall they turn orange like clementines, or red like apples, or yellow like lemons. Clementine, apple, lemon-colored leaves. Then they fall. Sometimes they turn brown first, but mostly they turn brown after they fall, and after a whole bunch of them fall, you can rake them into big piles, and when you're five or six years old, you can hide in them and be giggly with Maureen, the girl across the street.

But the main thing about autumn leaves is that they fall. No one can do anything about that. School starts, the weather cools down, leaves turn color and drop. School starting doesn't make that happen—it only feels like it.

Mom used to hate seeing the leaves fall, and once in a

while she'd wave a fist at a leaf that sloped first this way and then that on its way down from the oak tree out front and say, "You get back up there!"

Half a joke. Because she didn't like cold weather. Like Maureen. Maureen says she's cold from October to June, but I don't know how that's possible. I'm not cold all that time. I wear shorts when she's still in sweaters and long pants. When it's in the eighties.

"You can't be cold," I said to her one time in early spring.

"Why not?" she asked.

"Because it's warm outside," I said.

"Not to me."

"The air is just as warm for you as it is for me."

"That," she said, "is one of the late great fallacies."

So I give up.

Maureen. I guess I could be in love with her in another couple of years. But I don't want to be in love with her yet. I want to play run-the-bases with her and walk to school with her and just be friends with her.

Because Maureen—you just know where you are with Maureen. And even though she's gotten kind of funny since we started high school—wearing all black all the time and cutting classes so she can write poetry in the nature center or just not be in school—she's still Maureen, cutting through the junk.

Here's one of her poems. I had to memorize it when I lost

a game of run-the-bases to her one day last fall. If I'd won, she would have had to pick up a frog the next time we saw one at the creek. Oh, she did it anyway because she likes frogs. We don't give each other bad penalties.

Here's the poem:

I'm a girl
Who dresses in black
I dress in black
Don't make any crack
I dress in black
Watch your mouth, Jack
'Cause it's a fack
I dress in black

That's not her best poem, but she wrote it because I'd been on her about wearing all black all the time. I said, my name isn't Jack, and anyway, "fact" is spelled with a *t*. She said so what. Read some e.e. cummings. And memorize my poem or I'll make you eat dirt. So I did. Memorize the poem, I mean. And that's why I can write it here.

Maureen.

Here's the thing about Maureen. You can have a big long argument with her about anything you want, be as convincing as you want—about pot, for instance. And after you're all finished, she'll look at you and say, "That's fine, but do you really want parameciums for children?"

And slice your argument to smithereens because she's put her finger on the one point you can't argue away. Not that I really smoke pot. I tried it once, and it made me sick. I felt awful all the next day too. And I thought it might help something. Boy, was I dumb!

And no, I don't want parameciums for children, but maybe I don't want children. Then, what difference would it make if pot messed with my DNA? But then Maureen would say either *Maybe you don't want children now, but you could change your mind* or *Why would you smoke something that made you sick even once?* And she'd be right, and you'd know it even if you decided to go ahead and do the dumb thing.

Well, I haven't smoked cigarettes since May. I haven't wanted to. I still have a pack with four cigarettes in it in my backpack. I guess. I guess they're still in there. They could be brownies for all it matters.

I used to really like brownies. Dad made some a couple of weeks after the school fire, and they just sat on the counter getting stale. I ate one, but I didn't care. Eat a brownie, don't eat a brownie. Whatever.

I eat what Dad cooks for dinner, and I eat cereal with him in the morning before he heads off to work. Sometimes he scrambles eggs or mixes up pancakes, but it could be mud for all I care, and I don't come in off the back porch just to make some stupid sandwich out of what's in the fridge and eat it. But if Dad's got a bowl of apples on the porch, I'll probably grab one once in a while and eat that. Eat an apple, sleep some, watch the cars that come down the lane. And there's the fence now that goes all around the yard, so you can't see the street or the woods as well as you used to. Dad says the fence will come down some day, but we need it now.

Or we might move. We talk about that, but so far I don't want to.

Because Maureen still lives across the street. I don't want to move away from Maureen.

7.

Today I'm writing about vanilla ice cream. You can sit on the back porch steps and watch the street only so long.

Vanilla . . .

I saw a new cat today. It was black with a white mouth, like it had found some vanilla ice cream and liked it a little too much. Probably looking for old Preston, who likes to stretch out on my sleeping bag all day. The new cat must have squeezed in between the gate and the post. How he got out of the yard again, I don't know. Maybe the same way.

Preston looked up when the other cat went through, but he doesn't have much energy for play anymore. He's good company, though, and he purrs a tune for me once in a while, just like the old days. Preston. I wonder if he remembers Mom. He must. He was her cat before she married Dad.

Two cars just went by. At least they went by. But I'm just sitting here. Preston's sleeping over there. A copy of Mark Twain's *Roughing It* is on the wicker table, staying in just that angle to the side of the table, not moving, since the last time I touched it, but I can't read it for more than a minute at a time. Then I'm back to looking at the street, and I'm *sick* of looking at the street.

Officially vanilla's my favorite kind of ice cream. Dad has it in the freezer almost all the time. In there between the broccoli and the pierogi. But one time Dad knew Maureen would be over, and she likes raspberry ripple frozen yogurt. So he bought that.

That's Maureen for you. She's not like everybody else. Most people like strawberry, chocolate, or vanilla. Maybe cookie dough or something like that, that's kind of a fad, but raspberry ripple frozen yogurt? That's not everybody. And she doesn't care if nobody else likes it.

She'll say when you ask her if she likes cookie dough ice cream, "Sure, it's okay." But then she'll eat raspberry ripple yogurt or chocolate strawberry or maybe she won't ask for anything but a drink of water.

Water. I guess I'm thirsty. Bye.

8.

June 25th

today the deal is all lowercase letters and no commas. e.e. cummings is a poet who wrote only in lowercase. he's one of maureen's favorite poets.

   this lowercase stuff is hard. i crossed out maureen's name three times to get it right and now there's a big blue blob in the middle of the page. i touched it with the side of my hand and now that whole side is blue.

   no. i am not going to say the whole side of my hand is blue and it matches the way i feel. somebody else would say that and it's so—so—i don't know the word. sobby sentimental or something. like soggy bread. that's not how i feel!

   blue. hah! there's no color to match me. there isn't a color that dark. it's not about color either. inside this hole of darkness are things that move and won't lie down—like invisible people in scary masks tiptoeing around ready to get you. you can't see them but you know they're there by the motion. you can feel them but you don't know who they are.

lowercase. that's what I'm here to do.

what i will say is that it's hard to write without commas too. i never knew how much I was used to using them. my english teachers always show the absence of commas with big red circles. maybe their absences symbolized what i wished i was. absent from school. but that's a stretch. they were just mistakes.

and now it's a reality. i am absent from school. i was. school's out now but it doesn't feel any different to me than it did when i was just not going and everybody else was. except m—hah! got the first letter right this time!—a u r e e n.

so, Maureen—

Oh, heck. I quit. Let the mistakes sit there in all their glory. I don't care. I was just trying to fill time, fill the page, fill my mind, fill the air, fill the universe with blue ink. I want to write so I don't think, and that's all I want. Move the pen around the page and talk about things like commas and poets who write in lowercase.

How did his English teacher put up with that? Even his name is always in lowercase in books. e.e. cummings. That's what Maureen says. How old was he before anyone let him get away with that? And did his English teachers feel stupid later when he got famous because they'd always made him use capitals? I should look that up. Maybe Maureen knows.

Well, I'm not writing about lowercase and commas and doing without them now. So I've used up my topic for the day, and that's it. I'll put down the pen. I'll put down the notebook that dents my leg with its metal spiral as I write. I'll put them down by *Roughing It*, pet Preston, see how much of *Roughing It* I can read before I sit on the steps and watch the fenced-out street. Grab an apple and stare.

9.

Pete. Pete was so funny. People thought I was the funny one, but Pete could crack me up like nobody else. He could look across the room at me, and I'd laugh.

"What are you laughing at?" he'd say, all serious. All serious with that smallest of small challenges in his face. And voice. Then I'd have to laugh some more. It wasn't what he said. It was him. Just his delivery and the look on his face. That seriousness that went a sixteenth of an inch over the edge.

Once, at lunch, he said to Carl, the boy across from me who was new to the school, "Watch this." Then he turned to me all wide-eyed innocence and serious. He said, "Joey, the sky is blue." You had to hear his tone of voice. But I was the only one who heard it that way. The tone of voice and the expression on his face. Deadpan plus a notch. "Joey, the sky is blue."

"What?" asked Carl, but I was already laughing. He looked at me. "What's funny?" Then at Pete. "What am I supposed to see? Why's he laughing? Why did you tell him that?"

By then I was practically on the floor, and everybody else at the table was laughing. Like a big inside joke.

No matter what, Pete could make me laugh. When I flunked a test, when I fell off my bike, even the time my appendix flared up in gym class before I had it out. "Well, you know, Joe," he said to me on that day as I lay in agony on the floor, "they say it could rain." And I laughed while the gym teacher looked at Pete like he was crazy. Laughed and moaned at the same time.

Even after Mom died, when I didn't think anything was funny ever, Pete could do that. Well, not right away. He knew not to do it right, right away. But later. Some. He knew when I could handle it.

Pete.

Come on, Pete. Ride over on your bike and make me laugh.

10.

After that visit to Beverly, I slept out on the back porch. For some reason I didn't like my bedroom anymore. The pictures of the race cars on the walls were too big, and the windows were too small. I wanted to knock the walls down so the wind could charge through the way it did in Ruby-ruby's house. Sweep all my thoughts away.

So the porch was a compromise. Once Dad had the fence put up, he said the porch could be my room and I could feel all the wind there was. So I was there.

Not too much wind, but sometimes there was a strong gale before a thunderstorm, and I would stand in the middle of the backyard, putting my face right into it, feeling it pull on my eyebrows, my ears, my hair. I wished the wind would be strong enough and last long enough to clean my brain of all the brown gucky stuff.

But there was hardly ever any wind. Everything quiet and normal. Most days, not even a cloud up there to say a storm was coming.

Here was my over-and-over thought: I want a STORMMM! Well.

People pretty much stopped coming by to yell, although there was somebody every day that did something. Threw garbage in our yard or chanted for a while. Until they got tired. That's when I moved to the other side of the back porch. They couldn't know I was there if they couldn't see me.

It was pretty bad there for a while, though, with people chanting and chanting like they were in a chorus or something. "Murderer! Murderer!" It seemed like half the town was out there yelling and screaming.

The first day it happened, I went down to the basement and climbed under the oil tank. Squeezed under the oil tank. Squeezed under there with a blanket and covered myself up so nobody could have seen me if they'd gotten past Dad to find me, but I still heard the chant and the rocks that hit the house, breaking the window in the front door. That's when the police finally got here and made everybody leave. Leaving us with a broken window. Window! The whole door was cracked.

I didn't come out from under the oil tank for two hours. After that the gray hole I lived in felt so deep and dark, I could hardly see the sky overhead. Who knew this kind of thing could happen?

That was when Dad sent me to stay with Ruby-ruby and Albert. Dad sat on the front step the whole time I was away, making sure nothing happened to the house. I know he did because that was what Maureen told me later.

"He was sitting out there every time I looked over," she said. "Sitting there with his laptop and a baseball bat." She saw that from behind the fence her mom put up, because she was getting it too. Although, I didn't think she ever came down from the second floor at all until things got a little calmer. Maybe she hid under her bed. No oil tanks on the second floor.

I'd see her sometimes in that center window above the entryway and wave. "Look," I'd say to Preston. "There's Maureen."

And sometimes Preston would purr, but I don't know if that was because he saw Maureen or if he just liked me talking to him. How well can a twenty-year-old cat see?

11.

June 27th

Today I'm writing about the color blue.

It's the color of the sky, although people say the color of the sky is just the color of all the layers of air that you're looking through. So does that mean that the sky isn't blue and only just looks like it, or does it mean that the color of the air is blue and just *doesn't* look like it? Or is it both?

Blue. It's a good color. Mom's eyes were blue, but I didn't inherit them. Dad's eyes are brown, and I take after him except for my crazed black hair. His hair is black, but it's curly with tiny little curls. What there is of it. Black and curly on the sides and big eyebrows that scare little kids like a Halloween mask. Dad's all right. Not scary.

I remember my cousin Patty hiding behind her mother because of Dad's eyebrows. That was dumb. But Patty's always been dumb. I know she's my cousin and all that, but she's dumb. Being scared of Dad's eyebrows. For Pete's sake. You might as well be afraid of old Preston.

Patty would never jump into a pile of leaves. She wouldn't even ride a bike or race you to the corner. She never would, always afraid of a skinned knee or something, and now she's a cheerleader at her high school in Nebraska.

I don't know why I say it like that, like *see*? See how bad she turned out because she wouldn't race me to the corner? She's a cheerleader, that's all. Gets up in pyramids and stuff. Where'd she get the nerve to stand so high up in the air during basketball games? There are worse things than skinned knees if you fall out of a pyramid.

One time Maureen punched Patty in the stomach because she wouldn't do anything, and I was glad. I thought Patty deserved to be punched in the stomach, but I wasn't allowed to play with Maureen for the rest of the week because she did that, and somehow it was my fault. Maybe I told Maureen I wanted to punch Patty, and she did it for me. That's when we were seven.

Maureen spent the rest of the week digging a hole in her backyard, and when I was finally allowed to cross the street to see her, all this dirt was everywhere, and Maureen was covered with mud and smiling and saying she was digging to China.

"But," I said, "you can't dig to China." I was only seven, but I knew that.

"Yes, I can." She flung out another shovelful without looking up, catching me in the mouth.

I spat out dirt, mad. "Mau*reen*!" *Spit, spit.* "If you dig far enough"—*spit*—"you'll hit *water*!"

And then Maureen got out of the hole and punched *me* in the stomach. I knew you couldn't dig to China, but I didn't know she'd punch me if I said so.

How did I get to that from the color blue?

One thing about Maureen. She likes blue. When she was wearing all that black and dying her blond hair black and wearing black lipstick and black nail polish, she wore a blue pendant on a necklace. Every day. A solid patch of color. Darkest blue, but blue.

"Why?" I asked her.

"To be different," she said.

Different! Maureen is different, that's for sure. And it's not about that black Gothic stuff. It might be about her eyes, though. They are blue like the pendant on her necklace. The darkest blue, but blue. And they see what's true.

12.

June 28th

Today I'm writing about crickets.

They are so loud. *Chirp, chirp, chirp, chirp!* all night long. How do they go in rhythm like that? It's not a steady sound. The sound goes up and down, up and down, like the crickets are following a bandleader. How do their microscopic brains tell them how to coordinate? All that chirping keeps me awake at night. And then I start to see all kinds of things that go with that beat, and then I'm asleep with weird dreams. *Chirp, chirp, chirp!* Like the crickets are in some kind of band.

I've never been in a band. When a lot of the other kids were taking up trumpets and clarinets in the fourth grade, I didn't want to. All that squeaking and blatting all the time. Not for me.

I don't like music all that much, anyway. That's the real reason I didn't take up an instrument. I don't even like *good* trumpet or clarinet playing. Or guitars or drums or pianos. I could just write all the instruments there are and fill up a page. Write what I think about them and fill up the afternoon.

Oboes, violins, glockenspiels, horns, tubas, gongs.

But I don't care. I'm not writing a report.

Flutes, trombones, violas, accordions.

And it wouldn't be on music if I did. If I had to write a report, it would be on the *Maine* and the Spanish-American War. Maybe I will someday. I'll read up on it and find out what made it so important that Mr. Austen needed us to know about it that day even though the fire alarms were going and going.

No.

I don't like music. That's what I'm talking about here.

Castanets, kettledrums, English horns, contrabassoons.

If I liked music, I'd sit out here with earphones and listen to my favorite bands, but whenever I try that, after a while my ears start to hurt, and I throw the whole thing off. I don't care who the band is, I don't like the sound in my ears and the feeling of the earphones jammed into my ear holes. Same as with the crickets at night. No earplugs for me. They bother my ears. Just let the crickets make their noise. I can take it. They're only crickets.

But even without earphones, music hurts my ears. Not just my ears, either. It's something inside that gets tired. Maureen says it's the emotional investment.

And then she said all this stuff about music taking you on a roller-coaster ride, and how if you have a good ride, you liked it, and if you don't, you didn't, and if you're really getting it, it wears you out.

I just kept shaking my head the whole time she was talking like I wasn't buying any of it. "I don't like music," I said when she was finished, "that's all."

"But, Joey—"

"I don't."

"Jo—"

"I don't!"

"Fine, then," she said.

"Fine."

"Fine!"

And then I was mad, but I don't know why.

13.

By the time it was her birthday, Maureen's black hair had grown out so much that I could see maybe two inches of the blond. And she wasn't wearing black anymore at all. When she came over to my house that day, she had on faded old blue jean cutoffs and a T-shirt with dolphins swimming across the front. She looked thin with her jawbone sticking out more than I remembered.

Dad made tomato soup for Maureen and me just like Ruby-ruby did when I stayed with her. Tomato soup and crackers with chocolate chip cookies for afterward. And then Dad left us at the kitchen table to go read a book in the living room.

"So, happy birthday," I said.

"Thanks."

"This is the part of the year you get to be older than me, huh? Spending time with a younger kid."

Susan Shaw

Maureen pushed her lips into a pretend smile. "For a little while. If I can stand being with someone so immature as a fourteen-year-old."

"Ha-ha-ha. If I can stand being with someone who's already so old."

"Ha-ha-ha yourself." She reached for a cracker and bit into it. "See if I take you in my car when I get my driver's license next year."

"You're gonna get a car?"

"No. But I'm not taking you in it."

"Good." I nodded. "Safer that way." I stirred my soup, watching the steam rise into the air. "So how have you been?" I asked. Because I hadn't seen her really since the whole mess. Except for waving to her at her upstairs window.

"Okay," answered Maureen. "How have you been?" She lifted a spoonful of soup to her mouth and blew on it.

"I'm okay too."

Pause.

The air felt too quiet, and I scrambled for something, anything, to say. And that's not how things ever were with Maureen and me.

"I was thinking about that time you tried to dig to China," I said. "Remember that?"

She smiled, and this smile wasn't so pretend. "I would have gotten there too, if you hadn't told me I couldn't."

I grinned back. "Think so?"

"Sure. Mind over matter."

"And do you think China would have cooperated with that?"

"They wouldn't have known the difference. And we would have gone all the way through the middle of the earth and found out that they walk upside-down down there."

"I was going too?"

"I thought so. Until you told me we couldn't do it."

"You punched me in the stomach."

Maureen smiled again and shrugged. The real smile was almost there. "Oh, well. I *was* seven. Probably I wouldn't do that now."

"I'm sure glad to know that," I said, and her smile deepened, bringing out that little dimple near the right corner of her lips that you only get when you get a full smile from her. I was so glad to see that smile. For that moment we'd cut through the fog, and I was seeing the real Maureen, the Maureen I knew.

We just ate for a few minutes. The crackers crashed against the silence as I bit into them.

"So how are you getting through all this?" Maureen asked.

"Just living," I said. "Not doing anything much. Sleeping and eating apples."

"Sounds about right."

"How are you doing it?"

"Sleeping. Painting my toenails. Repainting my toenails. Digging to China."

"Huh!"

"And when I really can't stand it, I ride Mom's exercise bike. I'm on that a lot. I've lost fifteen pounds."

"Fifteen pounds?"

"Yeah."

"You look thin."

"So do you."

"Well, I'm not real hungry this summer," I said. "It's too hot to eat."

"Yeah. Too hot."

I nodded. "I count cars. But not many cars come here. And I'm writing stupid stuff in a journal. Just nowhere stuff so I won't think."

"That's the same as me using the exercise bike," Maureen said.

"Maybe."

We started on the chocolate chip cookies, but I was full. I could only manage half a cookie. Maureen took one little bite and then played with the rest on her plate, pulling the edges off, piece by piece.

"You're not dyeing your hair anymore," I said.

"I stopped caring," Maureen said. "It's just hair."

And here's a funny thing. I never liked her hair dyed black, and I wished she'd leave it alone, let it be blond, but now I wanted her to dye it black again.

I'm a girl
Who dresses in black
"Blond is good," is what I said.
I dress in black
Don't make any crack
"I was getting to like the black, though," I added. I wanted her back the way she was.

"Whatever."

I dress in black
Watch your mouth, Jack

"Whatever," she repeated more quietly.

I wanted her easy wisecracking back. The *Watch your mouth, Jack* part.

"Listen, Maureen," I said, because lunch was over and I knew she was about to go home, and I didn't want her to leave with us not being right together. "I didn't do it."

She looked directly at me with those blue eyes that see right to the point. "I know, Joey," she said. "Neither did I."

"I know that, too," I said. "We didn't do it. Neither of us. And we know it. But we feel wrong together. Do we have to feel wrong together? Can't we be friends like before?"

"I want that more than anything," she said, low and intense. "Do you believe in me?"

"Of course. I know you've never hurt anybody in your life, and you never will."

"And I know the same about you," she said. "I believe in you."

"Is that why you came with me that day? Because I've never figured that part out."

"That's why," she said. "I knew you were right."

"And you were willing to risk everything?"

"It wasn't much of a risk. I knew you were right. I knew it. That's all. The rest of them were a bunch of fatheads."

"Even Mr. Austen?"

"Especially Mr. Austen."

Then I began to feel better.

Why did Maureen believe in me when the others didn't?

Because she knew me the way you know someone who hid in leaf piles with you when you were little. She knew me the way you know someone who argued with you about digging to China. She knew me the way you know a best friend whose mother dies and there's nothing you can do except be there, and you're there. (But Pete was like that, wasn't he? But not exactly the same, not enough the same.)

Maureen knew me and she knew what kind of person I was. Not the kind of person who stands up to a teacher for something little. Not the kind of person who sets fires and walks away from a classroom full of kids to let them die.

She knew.

"It is kind of weird that we got out when all the rest of

those kids stayed put," I said. "Sort of like we had special information. Like what everybody thinks."

"Everybody's stupid," said Maureen. "The other kids stayed because they were afraid of Mr. Austen and his loud voice. Anybody who's ever had Mr. Austen knows about that."

"I was afraid of him too," I said. "But that didn't matter. I couldn't sit still."

"Because you were smart."

"I'm not so smart. I was scared."

"Call it what you like. You were smart to be that scared."

After lunch Maureen and I went out to play run-the-bases in the backyard. She sure could run. She ran so fast, and her hair streamed behind her, glinting in the sun, both the black and the blond.

We ran back and forth, back and forth, until Maureen collapsed right between the bases, laughing. I dropped onto the ground next to her and laughed too. It felt so good to laugh with Maureen. I knew, no matter what, that finally we were all right together again.

The sun was shining, the air was warm but not hot, and we were laughing. Maureen's dimple deepened and deepened, and I thought about how much I liked her and how pretty she was and—

Lightning! Lightning! Striking us, striking the grass, striking the bushes, striking the trees.

Maureen's mouth was an *O*, her eyes so round. My breath came shallow and hard like I'd been punched.

Lightning!

Strangers at the gate hurling lightning. Hurling and hurling lightning.

"Murderers!" *Lightning!* "Murderers!"

"Joey," whispered Maureen.

Not lightning. Words. Words. Yelled by a bunch of people crowding around a tall, skinny lady wearing a hat with flowers on it.

"You—You're *playing*!" said the lady. "How could you?" The flowers quivered at each word. "All those people dead, and you're *playing*!" Quiver.

I took Maureen by the arm and dragged her toward the center of the backyard, far enough in so we couldn't see the people and they couldn't see us. Maureen was a dead weight, and her face was white and pinched.

"We'll just sit here," I whispered. "They'll get tired soon and go away."

Her lips were turned down. "I almost forgot it for a minute," she said.

"Me too."

"We know you can hear us back there," came the flower lady's shout. "Murderers! Murderers!"

"I'm sorry this happened on your birthday," I said.

"I'm sorry it happened on anybody's birthday." Maureen shook her head at me. "How did this happen?" she whispered. "How in the world could any of this have happened?"

"I don't know, Maureen. It's like a tornado that wasn't there a minute ago, and now it's gone, but it took everything down with it."

"Murderers!"

"That's exactly how it is," she said.

Then we heard Dad by the gate. He must have heard them from inside and gone out the front door. I couldn't hear what he said because he spoke so quietly, but pretty soon we saw him striding toward us.

"They left," he said. "Are you two okay?"

"Yeah," I said.

But I wasn't really. Neither was Maureen.

"I'm not a murderer," said Maureen.

"Neither am I," I said.

Dad frowned and shook his head. "They're a bunch of morons," he said. "Try not to pay attention." Then he took a lawn chair and sat in it under the beech tree in the back corner of the yard. Just sat there. I knew the bees and the mosquitoes were bugging him like they always did, but he stayed right there.

14.

July 2nd

Maureen went away with her mother this morning. No big deal. They went to the shore, where they go every year. But now I'm alone again because Dad's at work. Alone except for Preston.

Oh, well, nothing's really different.

I'm sitting here on the back porch steps with Preston behind me, same as I was before Maureen went away. Same as before, I'm counting cars and eating grapes because we ran out of apples. Same, same, same, same.

Dad'll get some apples from the truck on his way home from work.

I go with him once in a while. It's fun calling up to the guy, "One Red Delicious, one Bartlett pear, a bag of red seedless." And he hands your order down to you, one item at a time, right out of the truck, where it comes from the ship in the harbor.

Right off the ship that had been to Chile or somewhere.

Just food, though. You can get it at the supermarket. Nothing mysterious about that.

So I'm on the ste

That was close. That car came by so fast. A yellow convertible. Came by so fast and stopped with a screech. People talking and car doors opening—

I quick jumped out of their line of sight. I don't think they saw me. But I dropped this notebook. It was lying in the grass the whole time, red and obvious, and I couldn't go back and get it without them seeing me.

It was all right that they might have spotted it, I guess. They didn't know what it was, but it bothered me, having it sit there out in the open and unprotected. Naked and unprotected. That's how it felt to me. Naked and unprotected out there, and I couldn't do anything about it.

Of course, the fence kept the people away from it. I had to keep telling myself that so I wouldn't dash back and grab it out of sight.

Then the chant. God, I hate that chant! Why do people have to act that way? I didn't do anything wrong. All I did was save my life. Mine and Maureen's. I tried to save the others, tried to get them to listen, but I couldn't. I couldn't. Couldn't.

Sometimes I wish I had died in the fire too. Let us all have died. Then no one would think I started it. Let it be twenty-six dead and no survivors. Sometimes I feel that way. Or twenty-five. Not Maureen, too.

But why did anybody have to die? Why can't we still be just ordinary? Kids with cowlicks and smart-aleck answers. Being what Ruby-ruby calls fresh. Why can't we still be kids that laugh and tell on one another and groan together over a theme assignment? Why can't we?

I'm like a guy with a dandelion weeder in his hands. The metal two-pronged thing. You push it way into the ground under a dandelion plant, way down to where the root is, and cut it there. When you get the weeder in the right place, you can feel it—*chherrrrunt*! Not a dry sound, exactly.

That'll kill the weed. But you have to go deep. Then you pull this long thing out of the ground and throw it away. If you don't, it could reroot itself. That's what my mother said. Was she right? Can a dandelion really reroot itself?

But that's me, the guy with the dandelion weeder. I need to go way under the surface, find the root, and kill it. Then Maureen and I will be all right again. But how can I do that? The building burned down, and no one knows why. Twenty-four dead and two survivors.

I'm sitting on the steps again, trying to write, but my hands are all shaky. Forget the blue lines.

15.

July 7ᵗʰ

Baseball.

I used to play baseball. I was pretty good with bunts, and in Little League no one expects a kid to bunt. Everybody always wants to hit a home run, so they strike out from trying too hard. Hardly anyone ever hits a home run in third grade. Because that's what grade I was in when I was playing baseball.

I could bunt pretty well, and even if I didn't get on base every time, the guy on base ahead of me, if there was one, always got ahead. See, what I knew was that if I hit a ball anywhere and someone had to throw it, chances were good that the ball would go over the head of the first baseman and down the little hill that ended against the chain-link fence that separated the field from someone's backyard. Eight-year-olds mostly can't throw too well. Or catch. Now if I played, it would be different. Bigger kids aim better. But still, bunters challenge the pitcher or whoever picks up the ball. A good bunter could win the World Series.

I don't know if a World Series has ever been won on a bunt. Maybe. Better than a walk-off walk. That's like letting the air out of a car's tires and watching the whole car just gradually get lower. If your team wins, that's good, but it's a pretty thin way to win. It leaves everybody hanging, everybody who was waiting for the big bang that's not going to happen so they can yell and scream and jump up and down the way they want to.

Instead, you go *Oh!* and then pick up your red sweatshirt and go home with your parents and have hot dogs or peanut butter and jelly before getting into bed because you're hungry and the game lasted past your bedtime. That part would be the same with a walk-off home run. You gotta end up at home. But the *Oh!* part—that's not why you go to baseball games.

That's the way it used to be here. We'd go to Phillies games— a couple a year. Mom would buy me blue cotton candy, but she'd eat most of it because I liked the idea of cotton candy but not the actual taste of it. Every time, it looked good enough to eat . . . until I ate a few bites. Then I handed it to Mom.

I remember her sitting there in her tank top with the big red *P* on it and her Phillies cap that she'd wear backward or sideways while she ate my blue cotton candy. Never the pink kind, because I didn't like pink.

Dad would laugh when I asked for the cotton candy. "You

know your mom's going to end up eating it," he'd say. "Callie, why don't you just buy it for yourself and give Joey a couple of bites?"

"Oh, I'm watching my diet," Mom'd say, and he'd laugh again.

Because she was skinny and always watching her diet. Except when I couldn't finish my blue cotton candy. Then there was no more diet.

I was never hungry anymore until we got home because those couple of bites of the blue cotton candy always took my appetite away for the rest of the game. Afterward, at home, that's when I'd eat the peanut butter and jelly or the hot dogs. If I didn't fall asleep in the car and get put to bed in my clothes. That's when I was really little.

Well, that's what we used to do. Dad and I haven't been to a game since Mom died. I guess we could go. The Phillies are still playing, although sometimes I feel that they shouldn't since Mom's dead. But what if we went and Dad bought cotton candy for me? He doesn't like it either. I don't think I would ask for it. That would be too much.

So, I've written about baseball.

Baseball and Mom.

Baseball, Mom, and apple pie. Isn't that what they say America is all about? Well, I didn't write about apple pie.

Time for an apple.

Pye.

16.

July 8th

I wish Maureen would get home from the shore.

17.

July 9th

Today's topic is cats. There's Preston, for instance. And there was the cat that came through the yard that one day. And then there are lions and tigers at the zoo. Bobcats and panthers.

Panthers. I always think panthers sound scary, the way they can just sneak up on you and pounce. All cats are like that, but the sound of the word "panthers" just holds all the scary stuff in it. I mean, there are no lions or tigers that run loose around here, so I'm not afraid of them. But panthers. We have panthers in North America, and sometimes people say they see them around here in Pennsylvania.

Panthers. Sneaking around under cover of darkness. Panthers, sneaking around just waiting for you to let your guard down and then—pounce! You're dead! You're dead and you don't even know it's coming.

One day you're minding your own business, maybe going to school or reading a book, and then *pounce*! It's got you and you can't get away and it's got you in its jaws and it's shaking you and shaking you and you can't let go of the bad dream because it's not a

18.

July 10th

This journal isn't doing what I want it to do. I sit down to write one thing, and another thing comes out, kind of like a wriggly snake a person might be trying to hide in a paper bag. If I'm controlling the pen, how come I can't control where the words lead?

I don't want to write about the fires. All those kids dead. And Mom. She died because of the first one.

So here's what I'm going to do. I'm going to write about the fires anyway. If I can stand it. Get them out of my head and onto the page.

Then maybe the wriggly snakes and the pouncing panthers will die.

Then maybe I'll be able to stop counting cars and start reading *Roughing It* and *Hamlet*.

Then maybe I will find some peace.

Here's the deal about the first fire.

I was there. It was Christmas a year and a half ago, and Mom and I were helping Gramma get things ready for dinner at the house in Germantown. Dad would be coming later because he was going to visit Ruby-ruby in Beverly first, so he wasn't there. Just the three of us and Preston. In an old house in an old Philadelphia neighborhood.

The first thing Mom did when we arrived—after giving Gramma a kiss—was pick up Preston and hold him like he was a baby. He purred and licked her nose.

Like always, Gramma said, "Your first baby." She winked at me.

Then we got to work in the kitchen.

Not long after that the smoke detector went off because some cookies burned in the oven. Gramma stood on the step stool like she always did and took the smoke detector down. Then she put it in the freezer. She always did that when she burned stuff because the smoke detector wouldn't stop just because she took it down.

That smoke detector was so sensitive, it would go off if Gramma was frying onions. It spent a lot of time in the freezer. I thought that was funny.

Sometimes Gramma forgot about the smoke detector and left it in the freezer until it was time to get some ice cream or something else. Then she would climb up on the step stool again, and back the thing would go onto the ceiling until the next time she was frying onions or some leftover drips in the oven started to burn.

The smoke detector went off that day because of the cookies. They were black like charcoal and we had to throw them out. Of course the smoke detector went off. It had to, with all that smoke coming out of the oven. Anybody could see that.

"I always burn the last batch," said Gramma, and it was true. I'd seen her do the same thing lots of times. And she always said that: "I always burn the last batch."

A while later Mom opened the basement door to go downstairs for some table decorations, and right away she backed up. *Smoke!*

"Out!" Mom ordered. "Out!"

And boy, did she have us outside, Gramma and me, so fast. I had a bruise on my arm for two weeks where she'd grabbed me.

Out on the sidewalk Mom called 911 on her cell phone.

"At least we're safe." Gramma looked white, staring at the house she'd lived in for so long. Glass tinkled, and then flames shot up from the window well underneath her living room window. "Oh, my house," she said. "My house."

Mom was looking around. "Preston!" she shouted, and she ran for the front door.

I started after her, but Gramma had me by the belt loop

below my spine, and she was strong. I guess that's where Mom got it. They both could have been championship wrestlers for all the strength they had.

"Callie!" Gramma screamed. "Come back! Callie!"

Mom didn't come back, and Gramma wouldn't let go of my belt loop no matter what I did, and I was fighting like crazy with her to get loose when the firefighters arrived.

"They'll get her out of there," Gramma told me. "They'll get her out of there, and boy, am I gonna give her what for when they do. Going after that silly cat. They'll get her out of there."

Well, the firefighters carried her out. It wasn't very many minutes, and she was still alive then.

Gramma let go of me when we saw her. Mom was burned, so burned. Gramma bent over her like she was all there was in the world. To her, she was. And to me. Mom, after all. My mom.

I heard some whispering between the two of them, but I don't know what they said. I must have known then, but I can't remember now.

I bent over Mom too, and whispered to her, "You're gonna be all right, Mom." Her hair was scorched, and black streaks ran across her face. "You're gonna be all right."

"You're a good boy, Joey," she said, and she touched my face with her unburned hand.

One of the Survivors

Then they took her away.

Mom died on the way to the hospital. So all we had were those whispers. And that last touch. I'm so glad for that last touch!

Mom got lost in the smoke and couldn't find her way out. That's what the firefighters told us later. When there's smoke, you can get lost even in the house you grew up in.

I write about the Christmas fire, and I know it was real, but even now, more than a year and a half later, it doesn't make sense. Mom—dead. How can she be dead?

Sometimes I think I'll walk around the corner and there she'll be, petting the Schwartzes' dog. Or she'll be sitting on the back porch steps eating an orange Popsicle she bought from one of those ice cream trucks that come down the street every day in the summer. And she'll give me one too, and we'll eat them together and she'll smile at me the way she used to, like we have a secret.

And I guess we kind of did.

But none of that's going to happen. Not unless someone really does invent a time machine and we can go back and change what we did. If someone would only invent a time machine!

Mom ran back into Gramma's house that Christmas to save Preston. We found him up in the maple tree out back after it was all over.

So.

There.

Now I'm going to count cars, and I don't care if they come or not. I'm going to count them.

Two blue, five red, and forty-seven black ones, all in a row.

19.

July 11th

Mom died, and that's the reason I'm still alive. Dad and Maureen are the only people who really understand about that. And Ruby-ruby and Albert. Gramma doesn't know about all this because she's still all crying about Mom way down in Florida.

Dad and I decided she didn't need to know about the school mess. She knows there was a fire, and she knows I'm all right. As all right as I can be.

But we didn't tell her the rest, about how everyone thinks I started it. Or Maureen started it. Or both of us together.

When things are better, maybe we'll tell her, but maybe we won't. Once you fix a faucet, why talk about when it was broken? If it works like it never was broken, why think about it even? That's what's going to happen to me. Everything will settle down. They'll figure out what caused the school fire, and no one will blame me or Maureen ever again. And we'll go back to the way we were.

So I guess I think I'm a broken faucet. I'm a broken something. Faucet, person, tree. Broken. Maybe a therapist could put me back together, but where can I see one? It's dangerous outside the fence. Who knows who you might run into in a waiting room? Better to stay put. Dad agrees.

Still broken, though.

Because I can't read for more than a minute. I can't concentrate. And I love *Roughing It*. I've read it five times. It's so funny! But I try to read it and it's just words on the page and nothing's funny, and my eyes skip over the black and white. Writing something is easier. At least as long as it doesn't have to make sense. My eye doesn't skip down the page when I'm writing. There's nothing to skip to.

If I can't concentrate, I put down this notebook. Then I pick it up again later. Lather, rinse, repeat. Over and over again. Because every time I start, there's still no skipping ahead. The last thing I wrote is still the last thing I wrote, and I add on from there without ever looking at what's already written. Like this:

1. Write something until I'm itchy and nervous.
2. Put the notebook and pen down.
3. Stare at the street through the fence.
4. Eat an apple.

5. Pet Preston.
6. Stare at the street through the fence again.
7. Pet Preston.
8. Eat an apple.
9. Pick up the notebook and write something until I'm itchy and nervous.
10. Etc.

Sometimes I draw. That works as good as writing, but it does the same sneaky thing after a while, and flames start to grow out of blades of grass or the beech tree.

The only thing that seems safe to draw so far is Preston. I try to always draw him, and stick just with him because he's safe. But eventually I always forget. Drawing him somehow leads to drawing the sleeping bag under him and the clapboard wall behind him, and then I'm seeing lines that look like fire or fire hoses or the blackboard in Mr. Austen's room. I don't ever pencil the fire or the fire hoses or the blackboard, but just seeing where the drawing is going is bad enough. Why can't I stop before it gets that far?

When it does get that far, I stop and run around the house five times to clear my head as much as I can. Afterward I collapse on the grass and feel my sweat drip into the dirt under me. And then I promise myself I won't draw anything ever again. But for some reason, I always do. Same as I always write again.

Dad says Mom would be glad that her tragedy kept me from dying. It kind of gives a reason for it. Well, not a reason, but a use. Because I don't think there's a reason. But here's the use—I learned something the hard way. I sure learned it.

I hate fire.

I hate bonfires, fires in jack-o'-lanterns, fires in fireplaces, fires in candles. When I grow up, I'm going to get a house that heats on solar energy so there never has to be a flame anywhere in the whole darn place. If there's a fire somewhere, you're sure not going to see me. If there's a fire anywhere, I get out. I can't help it.

But why—in all of the universe, why did this whole thing have to happen where I was? That's a question I'll never be able to answer. But I couldn't stay in that classroom. Not with all the clanging going on.

Here's what happened. And I'm only writing it this one time.

That was a dumb history class that day. It had been a dumb day of school altogether. You couldn't do anything the whole time except be interrupted by the clanging of the fire alarm all day long. They should have given us a snow day so they could test the new alarm system and let us kids stay home and not waste everybody's time.

Nobody could do anything, but Mr. Austen tried.

Between tests of the alarm he droned on and on about the

Spanish-American War. "Remember the *Maine*," he said during one lull. "Remember the *Maine* and to hell with Spain."

And here's what I thought about when he said that: I thought about Mom. She wouldn't have liked that—Mr. Austen saying "hell." And then it was like I was silently talking to her, kind of giving her a play-by-play.

You never let anyone say "damn" or "hell" or even "shut up" in our house, Mom. You'd give Mr. Austen trouble for saying "hell" if you were here. He wouldn't be able to talk that way in front of you. You'd make him apologize. Apologize to the whole class.

Then—

Clang! Clang! Clang! blared the fire alarm. *Get out, get out, get out!* it said, and the play-by-play ended.

Maureen rolled her eyes at me from across the aisle. "Another test," she said over the noise. "How many's that?"

"Maybe it's the real thing this time," I said, not that I thought it was, not after listening to the clanging off and on the whole day. I was getting used to all the noise, getting used to keeping the twisting away from my gut. Getting conditioned not to jump each time. "Fires do happen." But wanting to jump. What I needed right then was to hear Mrs. Patterson's set speech about the clanging being only a test. Then I would have been able to relax as much as anyone could with all that noise going on.

Before Maureen could reply, the clanging stopped and the

PA speaker next to the clock spat static. Now I'd get what I needed, and I could almost feel the sag of my spine as it would go when I relaxed it against the back of my chair. *This is only a test. Sorry for the interruption.* That's what Mrs. Patterson would say.

I pictured her curly blond head bent toward the microphone. Pale freckles all over her face and the ones above her mouth shrinking and widening as her lips moved with the words she said. *This is only a test.*

"Attention staff and students," said Mrs. Patterson. There! *Crackle, crackle!*

But then chunks of the school secretary's message disappeared under the static. I squinted at the PA box, as though that would help me hear past the interference. *Silly,* I thought. *That's not going to do anything.* But still I squinted.

"Please disregard this alarm," Mrs. Patterson went on in her bored, unhurried way. So at least *she* wasn't upset. "This is another test of the new alarm system." Okay. Test. That's the word. I sagged back and let out a good breath. Everything was okay! "Please bear with us while we get things under cont—"

Clang! Clang! Clang!

"See?" said Maureen between beats.

Mr. Austen got a disgusted look on his face and sat behind his desk. He and the rest of us waited for the alarm's noise to cease. A couple of kids held their ears. None of us tried to talk. Finally the blaring stopped and Mr. Austen got to his feet again.

"I once worked in a school," he told us, "where the principal went berserk. Fire drills all day long. We'd just about get back to our classrooms before he'd throw the switch again."

The class laughed at that.

"How did anything get done?" Donnie Mitchell called out from one of the front seats. He scratched his head, making his sand-colored cowlick stand straight up.

That cowlick made me grin. Nobody else had a cowlick like Donnie's.

"It didn't," said Mr. Austen. "Not until they took the principal out of there in a straitjacket. He was nuts. Really nuts. Well, let's get back to work. See how much we can get done before the next so-called test."

Before anything else could get said, though, the clanging started up again. Mr. Austen rolled his eyes, and the class laughed. Then the clanging stopped. Started. Stopped. After five full seconds of silence, Mr. Austen opened his mouth to speak. The clanging started again. Then it stopped again. The class was roaring with laughter, me included.

I don't know how funny I thought it was. I just laughed with everybody—wanting to feel the way they all did.

What I really felt, though, was frustration and that twisting in my gut. I hated how all the testing was making me think about the Christmas fire all the time. Keeping me nervous, keeping me worried. When I constantly worked so hard against it.

Think of kangaroos, I said to myself, *think of Martians, think of—*

Clang! Clang! Clang!

Mr. Austen stood at the front, his hands on his hips and shaking his head. "Test on Friday," he shouted over the din. "Test on Friday!"

Finally the noise stopped, and Mr. Austen returned the class to the battleship *Maine* and the bugler who'd played "Taps" that last night.

"'Taps,'" said Mr. Austen. "They say the bugler played it the best he ever had, with all kinds of embellishments and fancy improvisation. Like a short concert. After he stopped, the crew had thirty minutes of silence. Then *boom*! All hell broke loose."

There's that word again, Mom. I notice it every time. Does anybody else care, or is it just cool to pretend not to care? And why is it all right for teachers to curse in class? Aren't they supposed to be setting good examples?

"How do people know all that?" Pete Vitti asked.

"Mr. Vitti," said Mr. Austen, and I groaned inwardly because I knew what was coming.

And this is one reason I hate school. One reason I'm quitting the minute I turn sixteen. Why can't teachers talk to you like you're a human being? I tried not to listen to what came next, but there was no way out of it. I would have had to leave the room to avoid it.

"You're supposed to raise your hand. Then I call on you."

Like we're in kindergarten or something.

It just makes me feel mad. And helpless. It's just another way of saying *You don't amount to much, and what's important isn't how you feel.*

Why do we waste so much time this way?

Pete raised his hand, and I hated even that. But what else was he going to do? He could have said, *Just answer the question, willya.* He could have done that, but he went back to the rules. Game playing. I don't like games. I don't play them, and I don't like them. I just want people to be honest and straight with me. When I quit school, no one's going to play games with me ever again.

Take two steps to the right. Pass Go. Collect two hundred dollars. Bow at the waist.

That's not the way it is. Life isn't a board game.

Not for me.

School games. Grown-ups pushing people around so they behave a certain way. Why isn't it more important to learn about history, get excited about a piece of it, get lost in it like you're bodysurfing—why isn't that more important than being reminded again and again that you are a kid trapped in a school, and don't you forget it. First take two steps to the right. . . .

God, I can't wait to quit. September fifteenth of next year . . . every day, no matter what happens, is one more day closer to that.

Dad won't like it. He says a dropout has no future. What's the difference, I ask, if I know how to read and can do math and all that stuff? What's the difference to a boss? But he says, "Look who's working at the car wash."

Which I hate because this kid down the street, or who used to live down the street before he quit school—this kid Erik Wiley—he works at the car wash on Lancaster Avenue. You see him there every time you pass by. Him in his yellow uniform wiping down some car. He's been there two years.

Well, I'm not working in any car wash.

Why am I writing about that? I was talking about rules and Mr. Austen. And I want to finish talking about the fire. Finish it and be done with it.

So anyway, Mr. Austen nodded at Pete, just like there was a script he was following. "It's important to stick with the rules, Peter." He used his deepest voice like he was some kind of judge. "Now you may ask your question."

I glanced at Maureen, and she glanced at me. She raised her eyebrows and shrugged while Pete repeated his question. I knew Maureen was thinking what I was thinking: *Dumb rules.*

Mr. Austen began his answer. "Not everybody d—"

Clang! Clang! Clang!

The class groaned with one voice. Nobody thought this was funny anymore, I could see that. Mr. Austen's eyebrows came together, and his face got red.

Why's he getting mad? I wondered. *Nobody's doing this on purpose.*

The clanging went on and on, the PA box fizzled static, and the half-drowned-out voice of Mrs. Patterson faltered across the airwaves.

"Thi—" *Crackle, crackle!* "Test."

Mrs. Patterson always repeated her announcements, but nothing else came over the airwaves. Not even static. The clanging went on and on.

What? I wanted to scream at her. *What?* Say it again! SAY IT A-*GAIN*!

Clang! Clang! Clang!

I waited for Mr. Austen to tell us to line up—to make quietly and rapidly for the exit at the foot of the nearby stairs. Because it could be a fire, after all. How could we know otherwise? *Clang! Clang! Clang!*

"All right, class. I give up." Good. We're on our way. Mr. Austen raised his voice over the noise. "Turn in your texts to page four hundred and nine. We'll test your powers of concentration."

What? We're not going?

Clang! Clang! Clang!

Is he crazy?

Clang! Clang! Clang!

That uncertain fear had me in its grip, ramping up and up. My stomach twisted so much, I had to stand. I couldn't help it. "I'm sorry," I said. I glanced around at all the other kids. "I have to go."

I felt awkward and nervous under Mr. Austen's glare, but the smell of soot was all over me. The burned clothes still hanging in the basement afterward and the sooty smell and the wet carpets . . .

A lump the size of a tennis ball strangled my throat. "Sorry," I squeaked over the lump. Because he was the teacher and I was a skinny little fourteen-year-old kid with a voice that didn't know what it was. I wished I was twenty-two with a voice of thunder to match Mr. Austen's. He would have listened to me then. Wouldn't he?

"It's another test," said Mr. Austen, and his voiced resonated like a lion's roar between my ears. "Mrs. Patterson said so."

My palms started to sweat.

"I don't care," I blurted out. Panic now, that's what it was. Not an uncertain anything. Full out-and-out panic. "I have to get out of here."

The other students stirred in their places. Two stood. Cheryl and Jamaal. Maureen stood up too.

This was the critical moment. There were almost four survivors. Why didn't they hang on just for one more minute? If they had hung on, maybe others would have come. Maybe then it would have worked out okay. We still had time then. Then.

Why does a moment have to be so short?

"Sit!" roared Mr. Austen, like a lion with a rebellion on his hands. Maybe that's how he saw it. "Sit or get a detention!"

Cheryl and Jamaal sat again, their eyes turned down. They looked smaller, like they'd lost their bones or their muscles. Then *h-h-h-h-h*—That's not right. It was something like that. *H-h-h-h-* or *ph-ph-ph-ph-* or *chchchchch*—I can hear it in my head, but I can't bring it down onto the page.

It was an odd noise that came from the other kids between beats of the alarm. Not quite a hiss. Bordering on a sigh. I still wonder what it was.

In all that, I hadn't moved. I was still standing there. Everybody stared at me with wondering looks on their faces. Right now it feels like they were supporting me, telling me silently to do what they couldn't do themselves. Like they were already dead and trying to save me. It couldn't have been that. They weren't dead and they couldn't have known they were about to be. Maybe after a person dies, whoever's left paints wings on them. On what they were.

I almost remember seeing the wings, but I think I'm out of my mind. I don't think I know what I'm thinking half the time. My brain's on Mars. Or Neptune. Or in the next galaxy.

That time I was standing along the Delaware when Albert came to find me—like I was in a trance. If he hadn't come for me, maybe I'd still be standing there, turned to a statue.

What *is* this?

Why can't I think?

20.

July 12th

I'm going to finish writing about the school fire and then be done with it. Finish and move on.

Here's what was next. Me still standing in that classroom. I felt so desperate standing there. Mr. Austen with his angry lion's eyes, speaking in his angry lion's voice, telling Maureen and me not to do what I knew we just had to do, what we *all* had better do, the other kids watching to see which way we would go, and us just standing there.

Seconds were ticking by. Who knew how much time we had? That is, if there *was* a fire, which I wasn't sure of. I just was scared that there was. Because that's how I'm made since Mom died. Scared to death of fire.

That was the main thing. I was scared. Scared.

Somehow, the room felt quiet. The noise from the alarm,

the kids looking at me, Mr. Austen, red in the face, yelling. So noisy, and yet I only heard silence. How does that make sense? But that's how I remember it. Just a lot of shiny white silence.

I started for the door, walking through the aisles of turned-up heads. I was doing something different. I was going to get in so much trouble, but I couldn't help it. The house burning and the smell of soot—

"I'm coming with you, Joey." Maureen's voice was soft. How did I hear that soft voice through that shiny white silence? I turned to see her following me up the aisle.

"Maureen. Joseph." Mr. Austen's angry lion's eyes pierced the silvery whiteness. That's what it was—more his eyes than his roar. Angry and hard. But the roar was there too. "Take your seats. Take your seats or take detentions."

Maureen opened the door and softly slipped from the room. She didn't answer or even look back.

"I'm sorry, Mr. Austen," I said. "My mother died in a fire last year, and you'll have to understand."

Mr. Austen's face went blank. Whatever else, he hadn't been expecting that. Did he really not know, though? Don't they tell teachers things like that? But he didn't say anything. Not *Oh, I'm sorry.* Or *Then, go ahead. Do what you have to do.* Or even *Sit down. I'm the boss. I know what I'm doing.*

If he'd only said something, maybe I'd have stayed. Kept my pride and stayed. Or left but felt like he understood. And that way, maybe some of the other kids would have come with me. Maybe all of them. Mr. Austen, too. Because he would have gotten it.

But he said nothing. The alarm still blared, and I didn't know what to do but keep going. Because he said nothing. And the smell of soot had me covered in black. Why did he say nothing?

At the doorway I looked back at the room. Donnie slouching in the front, crossing his eyes at me. Pete looking mad with his chin out. Priscilla biting her lip and with her black hair all spiky with its purple points. The pink stuffed elephant in the back of the room, borrowed from Simone's little sister as a prop for Simone's oral report. The easel that leaned against the wall left over from that one day the art teacher covered Mr. Austen's classes . . .

My brain took a shapshot of the room and all the kids in it before I joined Maureen in the deserted hall. She nodded, and we walked together, taking the few steps on the shiny brown floor that led from room E201 to the staircase.

There.

21.

July 13th

I took that snapshot out of my head and made a drawing of it. It's leaning against the outside of the house next to the sliding glass door, where I can see it if I turn my head. Preston sniffed it when I put it there and then curled up on that sunny patch in front of it, and that's where he still is. Dad says maybe he'll get the sketch framed, but right now I don't care. It's fine where it is.

22.

Dad lent me his laptop so I could look up the *Maine* out on the porch. See if I could figure out what was so important about it that Mr. Austen lost his mind over making sure our class knew about it. And lost his life.

At 9:10 p.m. on February 15, 1898, a bugler named C. H. Newton played "Taps." Captain Charles D. Sigsbee, the captain of the ship, was writing a letter to his wife, and the music coming out of Newton's bugle with its embellishments and improvisations was so amazing, he stopped writing to listen.

Afterward, the bugler went belowdecks, where he slept. The captain finished his letter, and a couple of lieutenants joked together by the railing as they looked at the lights of Havana. They were still joking at 9:40.

Then—

BANG! The ship sank, and most of the people on board died.

I bet people on all the ships in the harbor heard that last "Taps." I bet some of them leaned against their ship's railing while they listened, soaking in every note, wishing the bugler would play on and on, glad that they'd get another chance to listen the next night. The promise of the every-night bugler.

C. H. Newton. That was all I could find out about the bugler. His name. Maybe somewhere there was more information than that. What was his first name? How old was he? Where was he from? Was he married? Did he have kids? And where did he learn to play like that?

Maybe all that didn't matter. A half hour after he played, the ship exploded and he died, just like most of the men on the ship. He died, and when in 1910 the Army Corp of Engineers put a cofferdam around the *Maine* and pumped the water away from it, they found the bugle. They also found forty bodies still in the ship. Forty bodies. Maybe one of them was C. H. Newton.

I thought it mattered who C. H. Newton was. I thought it mattered that the last wonderful thing most of those guys had in their lives was C. H. Newton's final rendition of "Taps." And I thought it mattered that the promise of his playing was destroyed by the explosion.

All right. The facts.

The battleship *Maine* blew up in a Cuban harbor, and the United States pretended that it was an act of war by the

Spanish. We completely ignored the lack of proof, the newspapers lied all over the place, and, basically, we just wanted war with Spain.

This made me think of *Hamlet*. And the school fire.

I didn't set that school fire, and neither did Maureen, and there were no facts that said that we did. But that didn't stop people from saying we did it. That didn't stop people from chanting and throwing garbage over the fence.

No proof of murder existed in King Hamlet's death. Before Hamlet went around blaming Claudius, he should have had *facts*.

Yellow journalism, hysteria, lies. That's what it was with the *Maine*. Hardly anybody wanted to look at the truth. They didn't care. They just wanted to feel outraged and fight. But what about the Spanish people who died for no reason? What about that? No proof existed anywhere that the *Maine*'s explosion was an act of aggression. Ever. People just wanted a war. They should have had *facts*!

I read that one piece of proof that something had hit the boat from the outside would have been a geyser of water thrown high into the air. No one saw a geyser of water.

Another piece of proof would have been a bunch of dead fish floating in the harbor the next morning. No dead fish.

The answer to the mystery was awful, and no wonder people in this country didn't want to hear it. We did it—us.

Killed our own sailors with a poorly designed ship. Who would burn coal right next to a load of ammo? I knew better than that when I was four years old.

The more I read about the *Maine* and what happened afterward, the more I saw myself on the *Alfonso XII* with the school fire leaping toward the sky behind me. The *Alfonso XII*—the Spanish cruiser that came to our sailors' rescue. Good guys that helped us when we blew ourselves up. And how did we repay them?

A bunch of battleships built around the same time as the *Maine* had coal bunkers in the same place as the *Maine's*—right next to their ammo rooms. *Right next to them!* Whose dumb idea was that? Didn't anybody ever look at the blueprints before they built those boats? Didn't they know what a magazine was for? Didn't they care that people would probably die? *Would* die? Because of bad design? Morons!

Some of the other ships had had fires before the *Maine* explosion, some of them pretty bad. Why didn't anybody learn from them?

In 1976 the U.S. Navy looked into what happened to the *Maine*, and they said the ship blew itself up. If we didn't absolutely know it back in 1898, we were pretty close to being sure.

Almost sure and no proof to point otherwise. But was that enough? No. We wanted a different answer so we could justify a war. We wanted a war. Who would want a war? Who would want all that death?

That war was the stupidest thing in the whole world.

I read about it, and I couldn't think of any reason why it was so important that because of it someone all these years later should have had to write the headline:

24 DEAD, 2 SURVIVORS

And I felt Spanish.

23.

Dad was playing something on the stereo one day when I went in for dinner. Dad wouldn't eat outside, but I could make myself go inside long enough to eat dinner with him if I knew that any second I could go out the sliding glass door to the porch. It helped to see through the sliding glass door, see the porch with the porch swing, and the wicker table with the backyard spread out behind all of it. Sometimes, in the middle of dinner, if I felt too edgy, I took a breather out there.

As soon as dinner was over, that was where I went, right away, sucking in that night air as far down as it would go. Afterward, back inside to help clean up the dishes. Then outside again, taking in as much of that summer air as I could get. At least I could do that.

Dad wouldn't eat outside, not the way the bugs pestered him.

"I'm sweet meat," he'd said once.

"You sure are," Mom had answered.

And—

Well, anyway, I went in for dinner that night, and something on the stereo caught my attention.

"What's that?" I asked.

"What's what?" Dad tossed the salad.

"The music."

"That's the Atterberg Sixth Symphony."

The soaring flute, the answering horn. It felt like a warm blanket. I went to the living room to hear the music better. A warm salve was what it was, and I could just feel my whole body go *Ahhh!* I closed my eyes and leaned against it with the *Ahhh!* The warmth of the tones all put together—

"Dinner, Joey." Dad touched my shoulder.

"Can I turn up the sound? So we can hear it better in the kitchen?"

"Sure, son."

So we ate dinner in the kitchen with the music following us from the living room. Haddock and salad and rice. Lemon bars for dessert. Good food like always, but I didn't care about it, except I made sure to eat decent at dinner so Dad wouldn't worry and talk about coming home at lunch to make sure I ate a sandwich or something. So I ate it, and the food was fine, but even better than the food was the music.

"Is that a new CD?" I asked.

"Not really. I've played it before."

"But is the music new? I mean, written this year or something?" Because maybe Atterberg didn't know about me, but maybe the way I felt since the two fires was in the air he breathed somehow, and that's how it made it into his music.

"Written in the 1920s, I think," said Dad. "Newish, I guess, when you think how old some music is."

Who was Atterberg? Did he know about the *Maine* and the bugler named C. H. Newton who'd played "Taps" that one last time and how all those people had died in an explosion? All that sadness, and wrong loss of life, and the going to war with Spain over something that turned out not to be true? I felt that he did. He must have. Because he couldn't have known about me.

So I borrowed that CD from Dad. He was kind of surprised because I usually just wanted to turn off music.

But this music was different—giving me that over-and-over feeling of salve covering every inch of my skin.

I found the old boom box under an army blanket in the hall closet, and I began a marathon of listening to the Atterberg. I played it and it filled in some cracks, and I felt a little better. Then I played it again, and it filled in some other cracks, and I felt a little better again. No matter how often

I listened to it, it kept filling in cracks, softening the hard places. And afterward each time, the gray hole I lived in had shallowed.

It turned out that I liked one piece of music after all.

One.

24.

July 18th

The Atterberg flows around me, Preston sleeps on my sleeping bag, and there is almost no breeze. Well, actually, Preston's not asleep. He's blinking at me.

Yeah, Preston, it's a nice day, isn't it? Warm, but not too warm. A perfect day for just being. To lie here in the shade of the porch roof and just breathe in the day.

I pet him gently. He purrs. He's so old, but he purrs. He's fine with me. About the only one who is. Thank goodness for Preston.

Here's what I want. I want to call Pete Vitti on the phone and see if he'd like to do something. *That's what I want to do!* There's a pool in Pete's backyard. I bet today would be a good day to swim in it. If I had what I wanted, I would call him and say, *Let's swim today.* And if I had what I wanted, he'd say, *Okay. Come on over* in that croaky voice of his.

One of the Survivors

I want that!

We used to swim in his pool. That was fun, pretending to be sharks around his little sister. She giggled and giggled. Her name was Sara and she'd be seven now. Well, her name is Sara and she is seven. It's Pete who's in the past tense.

I feel like I'm in the past tense too. What happened to that kid Joey? That Joey who used to live here? He didn't move away. He didn't die. He just got paler. He will never all the way disappear. Just go by halves, but there's always something left if you divide by halves.

Two divided by two is one. One divided by two is point five. Point five divided by two is point two five. And so on. I could fill the rest of this notebook up dividing by halves and it wouldn't matter. You can't get to zero that way. You need a minus sign for that. Four minus four is zero. But I don't have a minus sign. I can only divide by half. So I guess I'm not going away. I'm just becoming a ghost.

Staying even. By half.

The last time Dad and I drove past Pete's house, the pool cover was still over the pool, and the grass in the yard looked like it needed cutting.

Pete's gone. I can't call him.

Preston, though, you're staying with me, right? You're not going anywhere.

The Atterberg soars into the skies. I go with it over the

clouds and past the moon. It lifts me, carries me away from my hole, fills the cracks and soothes my soul. Then I stretch out on the air mattress next to Preston and

It's weird how I can just fall asleep like that. I didn't know anything at all until Dad came in through the kitchen and called me. So much for the afternoon.

Pete Vitti's uncle played "Taps" on the trumpet at Pete's funeral—at the graveside. But nothing happened afterward. No *Boom!* like what happened on the *Maine.* They just buried Pete. For such an important thing, it was sure quiet in that cemetery. There should have been a *Boom!* The only sound was his mother's crying. Bomber held her like she was a little girl, just held her the whole time, both arms around her waist, like she was afraid Mrs. Vitti might fly up into the sky if she let go of her for a second.

I went to that funeral, but I didn't go to any of the others. Dad wouldn't let me. Not after we started getting phone calls.

Dad says that by the fall, people will figure out what caused the fire, and nobody will be saying Maureen and I started it anymore. But I don't know. They must need to blame somebody, and once they get used to blaming us, will they be able to stop? Even if real proof turns up that the fire was caused by mice or a bird's nest?

25.

July 19th

I'm dead. That's it. All this stuff about how the world feels wrong to me, how I can't feel—or if I can, somehow I'm invisible even to myself—that's the reason. Invisible, dead, not here.

I know, I know. I eat, breathe, all that basic stuff. Or is that an illusion? Maybe that's it. Because I'm dead, just like all my friends. Maureen is too. We think we're alive, but we're not.

That's why it doesn't matter that I sit around and do nothing all day. Dead people don't do anything. Their bodies just lie under the ground and rot. Maybe my body's rotting under the ground somewhere while my ghost hangs around this back porch. How would I know the difference?

I'm just here with Preston.

Preston—he's not dead. He's older than I am, and he's lost

Mom and Gramma, and the house he lived in for more than eighteen years. How did he survive all of that? He looks at me with those green eyes and purrs. Then I feel a little less dead.

Not dead. Thanks, Preston.

Counted four cars.

Ate an apple.

Counted three more cars and lay down on my back, staring at the porch ceiling. The paint's got little gray lines that run through it, and there's a spiderweb in the corner near the bushes.

And inside my chest it goes *thump-thump*, *thump-thump*, *thump-thump*.

26.

I stopped going to school. I had to. Dad said it doesn't matter. By the fall everything will be different, he said, and I will be in some school, even if it's run by him in our living room.

They didn't throw me out. They couldn't. Nobody could ever prove that Maureen or I started that fire. The fire marshal came right out and said that. He said they didn't know what started the fire, but he couldn't tell for certain if it was arson or not. And they would continue the investigation.

But nobody was suspected. He said that out loud. So did the police guy. He said it could have been something wrong with the furnace. But they didn't know yet, and they weren't certain they would ever really know. It was all right there in the newspaper for anybody to read.

But so were those letters to the editor, asking how it was that

Maureen and I got out. How did we know to get out if the rest of the class didn't, if we hadn't set the fire? And my answer, which I wrote but never sent, was this: The fire alarm told us to leave, so we left. That's what a fire alarm is for.

The fire alarm hit Maureen and me harder than Mr. Austen's threat of a detention. That's what I wrote. And I wrote that I was more afraid of a fire than I was of Mr. Austen any day. Although I was scared of him. Him and his loud lion's roar voice and cold angry eyes.

Maureen and me—we both got anonymous letters. I threw mine away. Some crackpot. That was what I thought. Same as the phone calls. I didn't say anything and hung up. Do that two, three times, and they don't call back. That used to work. But then when it didn't, I stopped answering the phone.

After the fire, when they crammed the high schoolers into the middle school along with the kids that were already there, Maureen and I went back to school, same as everyone. The two of us joined a different group's rotation because the fire had taken ours.

All day long I tried to pay attention. Tried to listen, hearing the first ten words or so that the teacher said. Then I'd go into some kind of half-world where all the colors ran together. Then—*snap!* I'd missed twenty or thirty minutes of my life. Then I'd get maybe another ten words before it would happen again.

All day long just like that. And every once in a while—*snap!*

This time—*snap*! I woke up from that half-world and everybody was staring at me.

"What?" I asked. From the way they were looking at me, I knew something was wrong. I looked for the teacher, Mr. Pavarotti, but he was out of the room.

"Murderers," said Becky Frome.

"Murderers," echoed Ed Wilson.

"Murderers."

"Murderers."

"Murderers."

I looked around the room for support. But I didn't really know the kids in this class. Why did they hate us?

"Murderers."

Maureen was sitting all huddled in her chair, white as library paste. She stood up. The girl on her right shoved her, and she almost fell. She didn't look at the girl—Ariel, a large girl with big arms and legs. Maureen's wide blue eyes didn't look at her, just at me, only at me, as she came forward.

"Murderers," said Ariel.

"Come on, Joey," Maureen said to me, like we were the only two people in the room. She continued walking, never stopping.

"Murderers!"

It had become a chant. "Murderers, murderers, murderers!"

Why were they acting like this?

"Murderers! Murderers!"

"Stop!" I shouted. "We're innocent."

And they stopped—sort of. Like the quiet of a wave that crashes on the shore before it gets sucked back to sea. But that wave comes back, maybe bigger and stronger.

"MURDERERS, MURDERERS, MURDERERS!"

Maureen made it to the door, mostly avoiding the pushing and shoving hands that reached out. Mostly, but one kid got her so hard that she spun around. "Come *on*, Joey," she called from the door, scared-sounding. Again she gave me that look of hers that saw only me. "Come *on*!" Then she left the room.

"Yeah, Joey, come *on*," someone said three rows over. A boy with black hair. "Yeah, Joey!"

"Yeah, Joey, yeah, Joey!" The chant built as everyone joined in. "Yeah, Joey, yeah, Joey!

I grabbed my backpack and stood up. I started to leave, but my way was blocked by four or five guys. Strangers.

"Yeah, Joey!"

"We're innocent." I backed away from the soccer-like wall formation. "We did not set that fire." Why did they hate us?

Smack! Something hard struck me on the cheekbone. A piece of chalk broke at my feet. Marcus Perry, next to the rear blackboard, smirked at me. I knew him from my gym class, but I didn't know he didn't like me. He'd never acted like that before. He'd even joked with me over a basketball play just the week before. Now he made a kissing noise with his mouth.

I looked around for Mr. Pavarotti. Where was he?

More chalk, pencils, pens pelted my face, my chest, and those kids blocking my path didn't move. I kept backing away, but there was nowhere to go. Harder and harder came the chalk and pens. More kids were getting up from their seats. They were closing in on all sides.

Sock! to my right cheek. With that sock the wave formed again and surged around me.

Sock! Smack! Hit! Tear! I reeled and turned with each impact. Any second I'd be on the floor.

"Please—"

Then a stronger hit turned into a grab and I was dragged by my shoulder to the door. "*I'll* take care of him," shouted Derek Masterman. Derek, senior transfer from Texas, biggest kid in the school. Football player, wrestler, weight lifter. I tried to struggle away, but Derek was big with long arms and I couldn't reach him. I heard the other kids laugh as I tried.

Derek threw me into the hall and came out with me, closing the door. I cringed on the floor before him. What would he do? With one hand he picked me up, and with the other he held the door shut.

BANG! BANG! BANG! The door behind him seemed to arc around his hand.

"Go quick." His voice was urgent. "I'll wait until you're out of sight before I open the door."

He thrust me toward Maureen, and she pulled me away from Mr. Pavarotti's room. As soon as I found my feet, I was running, and we were both running. Running, running, running.

Away from people who wanted to do to us what they said we'd done.

Kill.

27.

July 21st

Everybody hates Maureen and me because we didn't die. How does that make sense? If we'd died, people would be sad about it. It would make the whole thing worse for Village Park—two more people dead. We'd be part of that memorial the township is planning, and two more trees would have to be planted in the long row of trees they're going to put across the new park.

But we're alive. So they're mad, calling us murderers, wanting to murder us in return for something we didn't do.

Why hadn't we died along with the rest of our history class? That's what everybody wants to know. If we didn't start the fire, what told us to get out?

All I was trying to do was survive. Get out when the alarms kept going and going. And Maureen came with me because she knew me. She knew I wouldn't leave a classroom that way just to cause trouble. She knew I believed there might really be a fire.

Jamaal and Cheryl got to their feet, and I know they were going to leave with us. A bunch of other kids looked like they might too, but Mr. Austen yelled, and Jamaal and Cheryl sat down again. Kind of put a lock on the other kids with that.

Why did Cheryl and Jamaal sit down again? I think they believed in me. Believed in me enough to stand up and start to follow. And believed in themselves enough to get that far. But Mr. Austen yelled, and—why was that enough to make them stop believing in themselves? Why was that enough to keep the other kids in their seats?

Why about the whole thing? Why did this happen at all?

Why were they testing the new fire alarm like that? Why didn't everybody get up to leave when Mrs. Patterson didn't tell us for sure that it wasn't a fire like all the other times? Why didn't Mr. Austen tell us to leave? Why did he tell us not to?

Just so we could learn a day earlier than we would have about the *Maine*? When he, himself, knew he hadn't heard Mrs. Patterson say it was only a test? He had to know that. Why did he make that part up? Did he really believe that?

I don't get it.

Twenty-four dead and two survivors. What's the point of that?

It wasn't like Mr. Austen had secret knowledge. He acted

like he did, though. Because that principal he'd had in his old school had run fire alarms until he'd been taken out in a straitjacket—that meant the fire alarms we heard were bogus. Where's the logic there?

Here's something I've never figured out—why is it that we're supposed to believe that the grown-ups always know best? My mother ran back inside during the Christmas fire to get Preston. Preston's cool and all, and I'm glad he's out here on the porch with me, but that wasn't knowing best. Even Gramma called, "Callie! Callie come back!" holding me to her with a death grip because I wanted to go too, but Mom acted like she didn't hear, never even turned around. She should have turned around and listened.

Mom died on the way to the hospital, and Preston was up in Gramma's maple tree after it was all over. How does any of that make sense?

That's why I couldn't stay in that classroom with all the clanging going on. I couldn't sit still, knowing what I know about fires. They kill. Sure, everybody knows that, but people don't really know it unless they've been there.

Maybe we all would have died in that school fire if it hadn't been for the Christmas one that took her away. Then it would have been twenty-six dead and no survivors. Because I wouldn't have started out so nervous. I would have believed Mr. Austen, just like all those other kids. And maybe Maureen would have too.

But why couldn't it be this way: Mom didn't die during the Christmas fire, and nobody died in the school one. Why couldn't we all have had the sense to clear out and let the fire do its worst without us? Be as smart as Preston?

Well, it sure did its worst.

I survived. Maureen survived. That's maybe as bad as dying would have been, the way things have turned out.

Wasn't survival the point, though? All those other kids and teachers from the rest of the school got out, didn't they? Everybody's glad about that, aren't they? It's just Maureen and me who people think did something wrong. All those other people, they'd like to kill us—give us what they think we deserve. But *they* don't know. They're just going on what they want to believe—not what's true.

Did attacking Spain under false pretenses make the death of the *Maine*'s bugler better somehow? How would killing me or Maureen help anything?

28.

July 22nd

Maureen's back from the shore. Once in a while I see her. Sometimes we sit in the grass and talk. Or don't talk. But she's back, and that's the important thing.

Maureen with her white, white face and no black lipstick and no black clothes and her white-blond hair growing more and more out of the black dye. Wearing sweatsuits every day even though it's summer. She's cold. That's what she says. I see that sometimes she shivers, but at the same time, her sweatshirt gets dark with sweat.

She's cold, and I'm sick. Or I'm cold, and she's sick. I forget which it is. But she's the one wearing the sweatsuits, I'm sure of that. I'm wearing khaki shorts and one of the Hawaiian shirts Gramma bought for me. I wear that every day because I just don't take it off when I get into the sleeping bag. Unless

Dad makes me take it off so he can throw it into the wash.

Then I take a shower, and the other khaki shorts and the other Hawaiian shirt are already clean, waiting on top of the sorting table along with my underwear and socks. And that's what I wear.

Because it's Maureen who's wearing the sweatsuits.

Because she's cold.

29.

The morning of May 22 was the most normal of mornings.

Breakfast was pancakes and orange juice and a couple of eggs between two slices of toast. Normal.

Dad laughed because I drank up the last of the orange juice for the second day in a row. Normal.

"But I wanted it with my eggs," I said. "I was hungry."

"Yup," he said. "You burn it up, that's for sure. Skinny as a rail and shooting up like a cornstalk. Want another pancake? I don't want you to starve."

Normal.

We were laughing as I went out the door.

Normal, normal, normal.

It was cool out—the kind of misty morning when you know the mist is going to burn off by ten o'clock, and then, boy, is it going to be hot! So I was wearing shorts and one of the Hawaiian shirts, for what the afternoon would be like.

Not Maureen. When I met her at the curb, she was wearing her usual all black, including a long skirt.

"Aren't you going to be hot?" I asked. We turned our feet toward school and started to walk.

"Not until the afternoon," said Maureen. "And not too much then. It takes me until June fifteenth to get hot." She smiled at me with those lips covered in black lipstick. I always thought the lipstick made her lips look like strips of licorice, but I never said so.

After a few minutes of walking we turned onto the pavement that lined the school's bus loop.

Clang! Clang! Clang!

That's when *normal* stopped. Forever.

Clang! Clang! Clang!

An edgy feeling began to twist my gut. "A fire drill before school even starts?" I asked. I stopped walking, and so did Maureen. "Maybe it's a real fire."

"Nah," said Maureen. "It's not real." She tossed her long straight hair over her shoulder. Just that ordinary gesture helped untwist my gut. Couldn't be a real fire, could it, not with that long straight hair dropping like a waterfall over Maureen's back. "It's that new alarm system they were talking about yesterday, remember? It probably doesn't work.

Just like the new roof that didn't work the whole year we were in seventh grade and we had to walk around buckets everywhere each time it rained."

Clang! Clang! Clang!

"I didn't hear anything about a new alarm system," I said.

Maureen laughed. "Oh, Joey. You never hear any of the announcements. Always reading or drawing pictures in your notebook, but never listening."

"Why listen?" I asked. "They never talk about anything important."

"What would be important enough for you?" asked Maureen. She shifted her backpack off her shoulders and rested it at her feet.

Clang! Clang! Clang!

"Oh, I don't know," I said. "Maybe that school is out for the century or that people named Joey don't have to come anymore. Man, I can't wait until I'm sixteen. I am so ready to quit right now."

The clanging stopped, and Mr. Garcia, the assistant principal, called to us from the school's entrance. "It's all right to come in, kids. They're just testing the new fire alarm."

"See?" said Maureen. "I knew it was that."

"Me too," I said, and mostly it was true. I just needed to be told. "Nothing to worry about."

Maureen slung her backpack over one shoulder and we entered the building together. Passing the main office, we saw Mrs. Patterson working at her computer. She looked so bored. Why did she make herself come to school every day, I wondered, if she was really that bored? *She* could quit if she wanted. No law made secretaries go to school every day.

"I hate the way this place even smells," remarked Maureen. "I wish the school *would* burn down."

I looked away, hoping Maureen wouldn't hear my sudden intake of air.

"I'm sorry, Joey," she said. "I shouldn't have said that. I wasn't thinking."

"It's okay, Maureen," I told her. "I hate this place too."

"I wasn't thinking, that's all." Her voice was high and apologetic, and her eyebrows made an upside-down *V*.

"It's all right, Maureen, really. My wish is that the place would turn into a supermarket or a fruit stand or a swimming pool." I grinned at her. "Or cottage cheese."

She grinned back. "You have the nonviolent approach," she said, "although I have to say that that much cottage cheese in one place would scare *me*."

We reached my locker, and Maureen paused nearby while I got into it. *Pow!* The odor of old sandwiches and dirty socks punched me in the nose. *I ought to clean this thing out,* I thought. *But not now.*

Then Gary Chaplin turned up. "Well, if it isn't the Wicked Witch of the West." He lifted a corner of his upper lip at Maureen. "Mrs. Scarypants."

"Shut up," said Maureen.

I looked back and forth from Maureen to Gary. If Gary stopped now, he'd be all right. But I knew Gary wouldn't stop. He always went too far.

"Do you have a date with Dracula, Mrs. Scarypants?" asked Gary. He fiddled with his locker combination before swinging the door wide. "Or is it Frankenstein this time?"

Maureen shoved him into his open locker—

"Hey!"

—and walked away without looking back.

"Serves you right," I told him.

He pushed himself out of the tiny space. White scrapes marked his arms where the rough edges had caught him. "Remember me to your coven, fatso!" he shouted after her.

Maureen was around the corner by then, so it didn't matter what he said. Not to her.

"What do you want to say all that for?" I asked him.

"She's just too weird." Gary slammed his metal door. "She looks like a female wrestler in drag."

"In drag? Do you know what that means? 'In drag'?"

"Sure," said Gary. "What she looks like. She rides a broom to school, that girl."

I opened my mouth to say something, but Gary was gone on his last word, disappearing around the corner after Maureen.

"What a moron," I muttered. I closed my locker, trapping in the old lunches and socks again. Maybe if I just didn't think about them, they'd go away.

I was still standing at my locker, wondering if Gary had caught up with Maureen and what she was going to do to him if he did, when Colleen Draper appeared, dropping her backpack onto the floor at my left. *Bang!* She must have had something metal in there.

"An old cookie tin," she said before I could ask her. "I've got my note cards for the English report in it so they don't scatter."

I thought of mine all over the place in my backpack. I could find them all if I dumped it out.

Colleen wrinkled her nose. "Oh, my gosh!" She looked at me through a major squint. "What's that *smell*?"

"I don't know," I said, and I took off before the subject of my locker could come up. Maybe she'd think it was someone else's locker that stank. Maybe someone else's did. I couldn't be the only fourteen-year-old kid with old socks and lunches stuck in the back of one of those dark green metal cutouts, any more than she could be the only kid who organized her note cards in a cookie tin.

Things felt safe and normal again. Maybe not fun, but

ordinary and safe, right down to the smelly locker and the note card tin.

Then *Clang! Clang! Clang!*

Things started getting weird.

Clang! Clang! Clang!

My gut tightened. *It could be a fire drill,* I told myself, even though we'd had one for real two days before, putting a good hole in French class, which had been all right with me. Standing outside next to the flagpole on a sunny morning was always better than sitting through French class. So could all this clanging be the real thing? Was it different from the testing Mr. Garcia had told us about?

Clang! Clang! Clang!

My gut tightened some more. *It's okay,* I told myself. *Calm down.* I tried to make the world ordinary by picturing the toss of Maureen's straight black hair over her shoulder. But the smell of soot brought panic with it.

Fire, fire, fire!

There is no sooty smell, I told myself. And there wasn't. No sooty smell, no soot, just noise. But it didn't matter. I could smell the soot, feel the soot coating my skin. Hardly realizing, I ran through the hall. Outside, outside, *outside*! Gotta get outside to the clear air!

Clang! Clang! Cla—

An abrupt silence followed, but I kept going. Startled faces raised up around me like helium balloons on their strings.

"Hey!" one kid shouted. "Is there really a fire? Is that why you're running?" He pushed his face right into mine. "Is there?" I ran serpentine around him.

"Attention, teachers and students," came the PA announcement. *Crackle-crackle.*

And that was the whole problem. The *crackle-crackle.*

"Please disregard the alarm signal." *Crackle.* Mrs. Patterson's voice sounded bored through the static. "We are testing the new fire alarm system. Please proceed to your homeroom assignments."

With the announcement, I stopped running. Only another test! Roberta Weidner met me on her way out of the band room. I gave her a foolish out-of-breath grin. She frowned at me.

"What?" she asked, but it was more of a statement than a question. "What?" she stated, like *What are you lookin' at?* before turning down the hall, swinging her clarinet case as she went.

Great, I thought. *Now Roberta thinks I'm an idiot.*

After that, things went back to normal, sort of.

Why'd I panic? What was the point of that? Mr. Garcia had told Maureen and me about the testing already. The other kids knew it too.

I turned around and directed my steps toward homeroom. I pursed my lips and made myself whistle a faint tune.

It was only a test, after all.

30.

Here's what happened after I wrote about the fires. I had nightmares. I thought writing about them would fix something, and I had nightmares. That was what poking into that awful stuff did for me. Nightmares where people just sat and stared at me, not understanding me when I yelled "RUN!" And then I couldn't run either. My legs were heavy like they were made of wet cement. I was yelling "Run," and I couldn't run, myself. Trying and trying and not getting there.

And then there was the part where I was surrounded by orange flames. Tall orange flames like the ones I saw coming out of the school roof, only on that day it was one gigantic flame that swept the sky. Every dream ended like that. A wall of fire circling me, getting closer and closer until I snapped awake in my sleeping bag ready to yell and yell.

So I put the journal under the sleeping bag, and that was

where it went for three days. What I wanted was to bury it in the backyard, and not in some little hole either. It would have had to be big enough to bury it deep, deep down, all the way to China. Deep with enough dirt on the notebook to squash the life out of the fire stories. To put the right kind of finish to them—like a funeral would.

"Why?" That was what Dad asked when I wanted his permission. "Why do you want to dig a hole?"

It was a reasonable question, but I didn't have any kind of reasonable answer.

"I just want to dig," I said.

Well, he let me. Dad was cool. He knew some things without having to be told.

"Dig out there near the back fence," he said, pointing. "Dig all you want."

He sat on the porch with Preston on his lap and a glass of iced tea on the wicker table next to *Roughing It* and watched for the first hour. With bug repellent sprayed all over his skin.

I dug. I dug and dug and dug and dug and dug.

I realized after a while that the digging wasn't about the notebook with its red cardboard cover and bent metal spiral and the limp blue-lined paper attached to it. It was about me not being able to stand myself. Everything felt wrong and disjointed all the time.

I dug until I was tired. Being tired helped, and when I was

tired, I wouldn't feel so wrongly put together. But then after a while I'd feel all the wrongness again, and I'd pick up the shovel and dig.

Then, late yesterday, the sweat dripping off my face started to mix with tears. I wasn't exactly sure when that happened. One minute I was sweating, and the next minute liquid was dripping from my eyes, too. I was sniffing at first, and then I realized I was crying.

And for a while I still dug. I wasn't going to stop until I saw upside-down Chinese people or until the feeling of wrongness split open and shed like an old skin. One or the other. But then the sweat and the tears and the mud got to be too much, and I couldn't see what I was doing. I brought the shovel down hard onto my right foot.

That was it. If I hadn't been crying before, I was crying then.

I threw the shovel down, and then I dropped next to it, howling into the grass.

Because of Mom, because of the school fire, because Maureen didn't wear black anymore, because everybody hated me, because I shoveled an inch of skin off my foot.

Howllllll!

31.

July 27th

I want to ride my bike!

There's nothing like riding a bike, the way you cut through the wind like the point of a sailboat and your whole body works together like a song.

I went on a fifty-mile bike ride with the Boy Scouts a couple of years ago. I ran out of water and kept going and kept going and got to where one of the leaders was sitting on the tailgate of his car with a bunch of water bottles and snacks. Boy, was I glad to see that water!

Well, I can't ride my bike right now because of my foot. But as soon as it stops hurting, I'm going to get that bike out. Maybe Maureen would come with me. Maybe we could sneak out early in the day and ride to Valley Forge

Park. Maybe that's far enough away that we could get away with it.

Sneaking to Valley Forge Park. That's dumb. Sneaking at all is dumb.

32.

July 28th

I opened *Hamlet* just now. Some guy says, "Who's there?" And another one says, "Nay, answer me: stand, and unfold yourself."

"Stand and unfold yourself"? Is this really English? Stand and unfold yourself. Try doing that. I read the next line or so, but then a car went down the street and I had to watch to see what color it was.

Blue and white, but I couldn't get a sense of what kind. Not a van or an SUV. Too small for that. But that's the best I could tell. One thing, though, it didn't stop. I went around the side of the house to make sure it didn't stop somewhere up the street and have some chanters sneak up to the gate. That happened once, but not this time. The blue and white car just kept going. Good.

One of the Survivors

I picked up *Hamlet* again. A couple of watchmen talking, and one's about to go off duty when two other guys show up.

And that's all I read because my eye just jumped down the black and whiteness of the paper, and I lost my concentration and my place. I'll try again later.

33.

I got my bike out of the garage one day and pumped up the tires, checked the brakes. Everything worked. So when my foot wouldn't bleed every time I looked at it, the bike was ready.

Dad said if he'd been home when I cut my foot, he'd probably've taken me for stitches. I was glad he wasn't home. I got my foot to stop bleeding finally, myself, and I knew I didn't want to go to an emergency room where someone might start shouting at me. Same feeling as when we talked about me going to a therapist. Forget it.

Ruby-ruby called me the day before. She was cool. She called me almost every day.

"How are you?" she asked.

"Fine," I said.

"Riiight," she said back, and that made me laugh. "How are you really?"

And I said, "Well . . ." Because I didn't know what else to say. Great. Wonderful. Terrific. All sarcastic.

If Mom were here, she'd have something to say if I went in for sarcasm. But sometimes you gotta be sarcastic. Just not to Ruby-ruby.

I can come back to Beverly anytime I want, she said. Stay the rest of the summer, go to school with the Beverly kids in the fall. And I'd've done that, but Dad was here, and I needed to be with him. And Maureen—she was across the street.

Not that I saw her much. I didn't know what she was doing over there. Maybe we were both afraid to come out into the open and cross the street. That little space between our fences—anything could have happened to us there.

Maureen didn't start the fire. I knew it, and she knew it about me, too. I was sure she did. When would we have had time? We were in class all day. She didn't go to school early, and neither did I. Lunchtime? What about it? You know, you can't just walk into a boiler room, throw a bomb, and walk out. People just weren't logical when they said we did it. Something was wrong with the boiler. It had to be that.

When Ruby-ruby called she asked if I'd read *Hamlet* yet. I said only the first page and a half. I told her I quit after that. I knew what she'd told me about Hamlet's father and all, but it sure looked like a play about a couple of watchmen. Maybe Ruby-ruby was mixed up about which play she'd given me.

Maybe she meant to give me a play called *Hamlet the Second*. Maybe that's the one with the murder. I asked her that.

"I gave you the right play," she said. Her voice was sharp. "You read farther into it, young man. Even Shakespeare might need more faith than a page and a half."

"It's boring," I said.

"Naah," she gave me right back. "One thing *Hamlet* isn't is boring. You try it again."

So I promised I would. I read the next couple of pages just to keep my promise. It turned out Hamlet's dead father was a ghost. He came and went a couple of times without talking. It must be funny if you're in the audience to see him just show up and scare the living daylights out of the other characters. I thought I'd kind of like to see that.

So I kept on with *Hamlet*, reading a little at a time. At that rate I'd finish by New Year's. Better than not, I guessed. And Ruby-ruby would like it if I tried.

Well, the hole you could see was still out there. The one you couldn't see still existed, too, although I played the Atterberg a lot to make it shrink. I didn't have many weapons against the hole, but that was one.

34.

July 29th

I've thought and thought about why I can't stop writing in this notebook. It hasn't helped anything so far. Maybe it's because I haven't told the whole story about the school fire yet. I said I did, but there's more to it. Maybe if I really write the whole thing out without skipping anything, I will at least feel like I did that. If I still get nightmares and daymares or whatever you want to call them, that won't change much. It's worth trying.

I don't know why I'm trying to lie in this journal that nobody is going to read and I'm going to bury in the backyard or under the porch when I'm ready—really ready—to do that, but the thing is, I've had nightmares all this time. Writing in this notebook hasn't brought them on, but I'd hoped it would make them go away.

Nope. They aren't going away. All those walls of fire hemming me in. All those faces of people who don't hear me shout "RUN!" Me not able to run and them not knowing they should.

Here's the thing about that day. I was scared. Really scared. But on top of that, I was not all the way convinced that there was a fire. Maybe if I'd been convinced, I would have shouted. Maybe shouting would have done something. If I'd been sure about the fire. But how could I have been more sure?

I was sure enough. So sure that I was scared to where I couldn't sit still. Maybe I was sure. But how could I have been? I smelled soot. I thought I was imagining it, but maybe it was real. But if it was, why didn't everybody smell it?

Soot. I felt it covering all my skin and making it hard to breathe. And making me see Mom sooty and burned while I sat in that classroom.

Well, that's why I'm not sure what I knew. Because the stuff from the other fire kept coming into my head. Where did the imagined part leave off and the real fire begin? I wish one of those fires had been imagined. Both.

35.

I walked out of Mr. Austen's room the day of the fire, and Maureen was waiting for me out in the hall.

"Come on," she said, and started for the steps at the end of the hall. I ran to catch up. "When you do something like this," she yelled over the clanging, "you have do it fast. Don't talk. Just go. The longer you hang around, the worse it gets."

"I'm never doing anything like this again," I answered, "but thanks for the advice."

We started down the stairs, Maureen ahead of me by a couple of steps. The clanging ceased almost immediately, and the air felt like snow. I paused. What did we think we were doing?

"What?" Maureen looked up at me from the landing. "What is it?"

"Well—where is everyone? Shouldn't everybody from

E wing be on these steps?" I shook my head. "Oh, Maureen. We blew it. It is a test. Now we're in trouble for sure."

Clang! Clang! Clang!

"Go!" Maureen shouted. "Go! Half the kids are on a field trip today, remember?"

"Oh, yeah." I'd forgotten. The hallway had been empty when we'd come up from lunch. Just our class up there.

I followed Maureen again. *I'm a fool,* I thought. A fool. I bet nobody else is leaving in the whole entire building. Just us. And Maureen came because of me. Why'd I need to get her into trouble?

I paused again. "We should go back," I yelled through the noise. "Go back and face it before we get into real trouble."

Maureen didn't answer, just came up those few stairs between us and grabbed my collar. "Trust me," she said, before dragging me the rest of the way.

The door to the outside was closed, and I reached to open it.

Well, maybe we'll duck into the alley, I thought, *so I can get a smoke before coming back.* At least get a smoke behind that wide oak tree where there are always cigarette butts. At least do something wrong for the detention I'm going to get. And then I won't have to sneak a cigarette in the boys' room later.

I pushed the panic bar hard and held the door open for

Maureen before following her out into the bright sunshine.

Clang! Clang! Clang!

"Nice out here," said Maureen over the alarm.

We paused, looking around at the empty, empty playing fields.

"But where is everyone?" I asked.

"This isn't where the classes gather." Maureen looked at me curiously. "Don't you remember?"

"Oh, yeah. I'm not thinking too well, I guess." I felt the grin on my face stretch nervously against my cheekbones. "I walked out on a teacher. It's got me feeling weird. Like any second I might turn into an anteater or something."

"You're not much of a rule breaker."

"I've never even had a detention."

"A detention is nothing," said Maureen. "A place to do homework for an hour. Not terrible or anything. Pretty quiet, usually."

"I guess I'm a chicken," I said. "Now both of us are going to be in trouble because I'm a chicken." And a fool. I felt like I'd be remembered for the rest of my life because of being a fool on this one day.

But I wouldn't be remembered for being a fool. I was going to be remembered for being something else I wasn't.

"I think you're very brave," said Maureen.

"Yeah, right."

"I do. How many people really stand up for what they believe?"

"How many people don't get expelled from school?"

"You're not going to be expelled."

I gave her a crooked smile. "I'm sorry I'm getting you in trouble."

"I'm used to it," said Maureen. "Teachers don't like you if you wear black lipstick."

"Then why do you wear it?"

"I don't care if the teachers like me. I don't like them much either. Now let's get out of here. I'll show you where I go when I cut class."

I shrugged and followed Maureen toward the jutting corner of E wing.

I'm gonna get in so much trouble, I told myself. *Dad will kill me. I'll be grounded until the day I die. Maybe longer.*

I thought about where we were going:

Around the corner was the parking lot where all the kids would be standing if this were a real fire. Or a real fire drill. This was no fire drill. So the parking lot would be empty. Except for cars. How could Maureen and I sneak away and not get spotted? All that open space. How can you hide in open space? All it would take was one person looking out a window . . .

A test. A stupid test of the alarm system. Everybody knew

it except me. Even Maureen thought I was crazy, probably. She just came to— Why had she come?

I shook my head. I couldn't figure that out. "Why did you come with me?" I asked her.

"Shut up," said Maureen.

"But why?"

"Shut up and keep walking."

I gritted my teeth. Now she was mad at me too.

I'd only heard the word "test." How come that was all I heard if Mr. Austen and everybody else heard more?

I'd gotten so nervous and antsy sitting at that desk in Mr. Austen's room when I couldn't understand Mrs. Patterson's last announcement. Sure, static covered half of what anyone ever said over the PA, and people were used to listening through it.

Not me, though. I never listened. Usually what Mrs. Patterson said didn't matter to me. Always stuff about after-school sports or the math team or extra rehearsals for the choir.

Who cared? I went to school, did what I *had* to do, and left. No hanging around for me. No extra stuff when all I wanted to do was get out of there and feel free to be the way I was. Breathe warm spring air and listen to the hum of bees. Act like a normal person.

If only I could just get out of there and go to Wyoming

or some other place far, far from school. A place in the woods where a guy could sit and think and not have to do anything anybody told him to do. Ever again.

Why would I listen to a bodyless voice talk about choir rehearsals? Choir rehearsals when a person's mother is dead!

But this time what was said over the PA did matter. I had to *know*. Me, myself. Not somebody else for me.

I thought of all the kids inside who were doing what they were supposed to be doing, reading page 409, playing basketball in the gym, mixing eggs with flour in the cooking room. Burning eggs with flour in the cooking room. Burning them. Burning. Burn?

Wait. Why was I thinking *burn*? Something was—

"Oh." Maureen's soft voice made me look up. She'd paused in her step just past the corner of the building, her eyes raised toward the sky. "Oh."

"What?" But then I was next to her, looking, reeling at what she saw.

Fire!

A giant orange flame leaped toward the sky from the building. I stared dumbly at it, unthinking, unmoving. Then—

My class!

I turned around and ran. I ran hard for the door Maureen and I had just left.

"Joey!" Maureen shouted. "Joey! Stop! Stop! Joey!" Her shouts turned to screams, but I kept going.

I knew I could get up there faster than anyone else could. I'd get there, and I'd tell them. I'd tell them the fire was real. I'd make them come out whether they believed me or not. I'd *make* them!

I reached for the metal handle on the closed door, and as I touched it, I knew. I knew the panic bar was set against me. The handle burned against my skin while I pulled and pulled with all my might, but the door was as still as a boulder.

"No!" I raised my fist and beat the metal door with it.

HOT!

Hot.

I backed away, staring at my fist, at the door, the handle. Hot.

A hand closed on my arm, and Mr. Bednarik, one of the gym teachers, was there. I hadn't heard him, but he was there. Beyond him was Maureen, still standing at the corner where I'd left her, watching me and Mr. Bednarik. Two teachers were with her. Even from that distance I could see how wide Maureen's eyes were.

"The door's hot," I told Mr. Bednarik. My voice sounded funny to my own ears. "Hot. They're in there. My class is in there. The door is hot—I can't get in. They're in there. It's hot. We have to get in."

I put the front of my shirt between my hands and the metal handle so it wouldn't burn me, and I gripped it again with both hands. I yanked desperately on the burning metal, but the panic bar did its job. I might as well have tried to move Mount McKinley as that door.

The door was hot!

"The firefighters know," said Mr. Bednarik. "They'll get to them."

Suddenly the muscles in my hands didn't work. They felt like jelly and acted like it too. I pushed one hand with the other around the shirt-covered handle, but my fingers wouldn't work. They kept falling off the metal as if they didn't belong to me and didn't have to listen to my brain. The metal was looking funny too, all wobbly and shaky. Then it got kind of dark.

But the door—it was hot! *Hot!* Why was it hot?

"Come on, son." I felt Mr. Bednarik pull me away from the building.

"I'm not fainting," I mumbled. "I just can't see so good right now."

"That's okay," said Mr. Bednarik, and he kept leading me away. My brain acted like someone was switching the lights on and off, and somehow that made my legs want to move in odd directions. It didn't matter. Mr. Bednarik kept on pulling, and I kept on walking.

The door was hot! The door was hot! My heart beat with that shock. *Hot! Hot! Hot! The door was hot!*

Mr. Bednarik brought me to the narrow strip that held the flagpole at the edge of the parking lot. Maureen was already there.

The door was hot! The door was hot!

"They all know," said Maureen. "They know because we didn't come out to line up where we were supposed to."

Hot!

It made sense. *Hot!* The principal always made the rounds during a fire drill. *Hot!* I'd never thought about it, had just seen it. But this was why.

Hot! Hot! The door was *hot*!

Fire engines and ambulances lined the bus loop. How'd they get there so fast? Why hadn't I heard them? Orange flames licked the sky. I felt like I'd been dropped into a burning hayfield on Mars. Why had the door been so hot? Maureen and I hadn't even smelled the smoke in the stairwell on our way out.

Hot! Hot!

"They're not all going to die." Maureen's voice was intense. "They can't all be going to die."

Hot!

The fire had to have moved fast after we got out.

Hot!

I looked at Maureen, and her black hair was bunched up around her neck and all anyhow around her shoulders. I wanted to smooth it and let it fall like a waterfall down her back. Then things would be normal again. I half-reached out to make it happen, but then I dropped my arm. *Hot! Hot!* Smoothing her hair wouldn't fix anything. *Hot!*

"Firefighters are good at rescuing people," said Mr. Bednarik. "I'm sure we'll see your class lined up real soon. What that teacher was thinking—" He shook his head, and I saw the tightness of his lips.

Hot!

"Mr. Bednarik!" Mr. Garcia was beckoning, and Mr. Bednarik strode away from Maureen and me.

Hot! Hot! Hot! Hot!

Maureen and I watched the firefighters. *Hot! Hot!* I wished there was something I could do, wished I'd had the sense when I was still in E Wing to grab a couple of those kids, *make* them come outside. Priscilla. She was little. I could have carried her under one arm. Priscilla and Donnie and Rab and Irene and Pete . . . I could have carried two under each arm, three, seven. I should have done it. Carried them. *Made* them come out.

Why wouldn't they come? Why did they listen to Mr. Austen when they knew what had happened to my mother? That wasn't any secret. They'd all come to Mom's funeral.

Hot! Hot-hot-hot!

Then a firefighter came out carrying a body.

Hot! Hot! Fire inside the door. *Hot!*

You could feel the crowd hold its breath while the firefighter lay the body carefully—so carefully—onto the pavement.

Myrna.

You could tell by her long, thin body.

Oh, no, Myrna. Her skin, her hair. Oh . . . oh no . . .

Hot behind the door. Too late. Hot. Oh-oh-ohhhh . . .

Everyone surged forward to see, but the police held us back.

"Stay behind the line," an officer shouted. "Stay behind the line." That's when I saw the line. A piece of yellow tape. CAUTION POLICE CAUTION POLICE, it read over and over.

An EMT bent over Myrna, but I didn't see her move.

"She's just unconscious," I said to Maureen. "I'm sure she's breathing."

But Myrna was so burned. *Mom! Mo-o-om!!!* I squeezed my eyes shut, but I still saw what I saw. *Mo-o-om!!!*

"She has to be breathing," Maureen said. "Penn offered her a big scholarship if she'll start in the fall instead of waiting to graduate. She has to be breathing."

More bodies appeared. Simone's. Trevor's. Mike's. My head couldn't process it fast enough to keep up.

One after the other, the bodies kept coming. One every few seconds, it felt like, but it couldn't have been that fast. Bodies laid out like dominoes on the bus loop with EMTs bent over them.

"Who's that?" Maureen whispered once in a while. Or I might whisper it. Because sometimes it was hard to tell who we were looking at.

"That's Donnie," I said once, but I wasn't sure because his hair seemed awful short.

Then Maureen said, "They're bringing out Mr. Austen."

We stared just like everybody else as he was laid down next to all the others.

"But they're not dead," said Maureen. "They can't be dead. We have a test Friday."

"No. They weren't in there that long. It takes longer than that, right?"

But the fire was behind the door when I went back. And fire takes no time.

"It has to. Besides, EMTs don't work on dead people."

A car entered the parking lot behind us and squealed to a stop. Simone's mother was the driver. She got out of the car, left the car door open, and was running, running through the parking lot. She climbed over the yellow tape, and then, even though the police tried to stop her from getting close, she was bent over one of the bodies.

Oh, that scream! And then an EMT was working on her.

After that, more and more parents came, running and running. They seemed to come from all sides. Running and screaming and wailing. So we knew. At least some of the kids were dead. Which ones? Which ones?

The bodies kept coming.

"Somebody has to be alive," I said. "At least one."

"There's Pete," said Maureen. "See him? His hand is moving. Is that his hand?"

No. It was a piece of his shirt. Somehow, it was torn and waving in the wind.

"Pete!" I shouted, but he didn't answer. "Pete!"

I ran to the tape and stepped over it. I couldn't help it. I had to see Pete.

"Pete," I said to him. *"Pete!"* I knelt by his form. "Come on, Pete! Look at me." But he didn't move, and his face was all wrong, and his eyes were looking in the wrong direction. I snapped my fingers over his eyes. *"Peterrr!"*

Mr. Bednarik was there, taking me away from Pete. "We have to stay over here," he said, parking me once again by the flagpole with Maureen. I don't remember going over the police tape. Did Mr. Bednarik carry me over it?

"But Pete," I tried. "Pete."

"I know." Mr. Bednarik's face was pale. "But we still have to stay over here. We have to stay out of the way."

We watched a couple of firefighters bring out another body. And another one. Afterward, one of the men took off his helmet and ran his fingers through his hair, wiped his eyes with the back of his hand. All in one motion.

"So much smoke," he said to a fellow rescuer. "They never had a chance once the fire hit the stairwell and sent up all that smoke."

Everybody was dead. Every single one. My whole history class including Mr. Austen. All of them except Maureen and me. That's what that all-in-one motion meant. No survivors.

Then everything got kind of blurry—not in how it looked, more in how it felt. Kind of how it feels to wake up in the backseat of a car with the lights from the toll booths dotting your legs and the tone of your dad's voice as he says "Howdy," what he always says to toll takers, sounding like a wooden spoon tapping on the kitchen counter. Not feeling quite real in a real place. If that makes sense.

A hand grabbed my elbow, and I was yanked off my feet and into Dad's bear hug.

"Thank God you're all right!" He hugged me even harder. He looked over my shoulder at the lined-up bodies. "Good God! Good—God!" He was quiet for a minute, looking and looking. Then he said, "Let's go, son. Let's get out of here. Come on, Maureen. I talked to your mom. She's on her way home. I'll take you there." He glanced around, and I looked too, to see what he was seeing. Lots of parents showing up. Lots of hugging, lots of crying. Confusion everywhere.

We started for the car that Dad had stopped just anyhow in one of the lanes when he'd spotted me.

Tom Smedley ran from out of nowhere to stand in front of us, making us pause. "How did you know to get out?" he asked.

"Huh?" I looked at Maureen.

Martin Binder stepped up next to Tom. "One of you must have set the fire."

"Why do you say that?" asked Dad. His hand tightened on my arm.

"Because the rest of the class stayed behind. If you got out, why was that?"

"Yeah, why was that?

"Why was that?"

"Why?"

"Why?"

"Why?"

So many people. How did they get there so fast?

Hate was in their faces. A minute before, they had hardly known who we were, if they'd know at all, and now they hated us.

"Why didn't your whole class come out?"

"Murderers! Murderers!" More and more people. Kids, teachers, parents. "Murderers! Murderers!"

It became a chant. "Murderers! Murderers! Murderers!"

One of the kids reached across and grabbed my shirt. Dad dropped my arm to push him away. I looked at the kid. A blond boy with a piece of my shirt in his hand. I didn't know him. I still don't know who he was. But he ripped my shirt.

"Back off!" Mr. Bednarik pushed his way through the crowd. "Back off!" His football coach bark overpowered the chant. "Back off! Back off!" He stood between us and the haters. "Back off!"

And they did, but not quietly and not very far.

Mr. Bednarik stayed with us like a bodyguard until Dad got Maureen and me into his car. Dad started the car and took it the long way, around the side of the school to the back exit, driving away from the haters.

We drove away, but what I saw and heard the whole way home was a visual seesaw. One picture was that room in E wing filled with my history class. Donnie with his cowlick crossing his eyes at me; Priscilla with her purple-pointed hair, biting her lower lip; Pete looking mad. Jamaal and Cheryl, boneless, sitting down again. And that almost-hiss.

The other picture was the one of body after body pressed

against the concrete. Priscilla's hand in a way she'd never held it, pointing her thumb away from her hip; Pete's torn shirt. Cheryl's burned ponytail.

No, no, no!

36.

July 30th

I wrote the last part about the school fire, and I couldn't stand it. Just looking at the written-down account felt so bad, I couldn't leave it here. I ripped out those pages, took them over to that hole I'd dug out back, and burned them. I pushed enough dirt over them so I couldn't see a single ash.

Afterward I felt a little more peaceful.

37.

August 1st

This morning I took my bike out for a little bit. When Dad was leaving for work, I was standing there on the driveway, reminding him to get apples on his way home.

"Sure, Joe," he said from the car window. "If you get hungry, there's plenty of other food in the house. You don't have to wait for apples."

Then he backed out, and I closed the gate behind him.

I used to think that people who lived behind gates were showing off. Like they were saying their homes were castles and better than everybody else's. Now I think the gates make little prisons for the people who live there. That's what it feels like here. The gate keeps people out, and that's good if they're likely to do something to you. But it's bad, too. All this being alone is for the birds.

After I locked the gate, I noticed the garage door was still open. Dad gets careless about that now. It doesn't matter so much since we have the fence, unless we're worried about birds building nests or something. So the garage door was open, and there was my bike off to the side with the helmet hanging from the handlebars.

I got on my bike and just circled it around on the driveway for a minute. But you can't get that great feeling of a sailboat piercing the air by just circling a little piece of driveway, and I wanted that feeling. A light mist still hung over the morning, and I thought, *Hey, it's early. No one will see me. And with the helmet, even if someone does see me, how easy is it to know one bike rider from another?*

So with my heart thumping and my hands sweating, I pushed out onto the street. I did make sure to lock the gate. I didn't want any surprises when I got back.

And then I rode. I let that wind cool me and grab me, and I let my heart rate rise and rise. I rode as fast as I could, going in a straight line. Pedaling hard up the hills, coasting down. Like whipped cream, it went down easy. Whipped cream. I pedaled hard for the whipped cream.

I didn't make any turns, putting as much distance as I could between me and everything else.

Until I began to get tired. If I could have avoided getting tired, I'd still be out there getting the whipped cream.

I turned around. I wished I didn't have to, but where was I going to go? I was tired. I was tired, and my foot hurt, and I knew the scab wasn't holding.

I didn't care. Home was all right, and now I knew I wasn't trapped there anymore.

So.

I coasted down the small hill past the stop sign at the bottom of our street and eased into our driveway. I was unlocking the fence when a car whizzed toward me. I moved faster so I could get inside, so I could get inside before it could matter. Maybe it wouldn't matter. Most cars coming through just came through. But then I heard it:

"Murderer!"

I got inside quick and locked the gate, but not before the car, a blue and white hatchback, stopped. I didn't look back, just rode to the garage and ducked in there with my bike, glad I'd left the door open.

"Murderer!"

Crash!

I closed the garage door from the inside and went on into the house that way. With blood seeping through my sock, I watched between the slats of the living room blinds until the hatchback drove off. I stood there a long time, making sure the driver didn't decide to come back. Then I went outside with a dustpan and brush and cleaned up the beer bottles and cigarette butts.

I didn't bother to call Dad, didn't bother to call the police. What were they going to do? A blue and white hatchback. How many blue and white hatchbacks are there?

But even with all that, I didn't feel *too* bad. I'd been out on my bike, so I wasn't a prisoner anymore.

The scab on my foot opened a little, that's true, and there was blood on my sock. So what? I cleaned it up and put on a new bandage. Big deal.

And sure. Someone else stank, calling me a murderer and throwing trash over the gate.

But I'm not the one who stank.

38.

I was on the porch when Dad brought the door home.

"Look at this," he said.

I went around to the side where Dad was pointing. A door just like our front door leaned against the side of the house. Except this one was green, and ours was white. White and cracked with the window covered with cardboard to keep out the bugs.

"You bought a green one?" I asked. "It doesn't look new at all." The green paint was scratched in places, and smudgy fingerprints blackened the center of one of the edges.

"It's not," said Dad. "Someone about six blocks away was throwing it out in his trash. It's a free door, and there's nothing wrong with it. I measured it, and it's perfect."

"Except for being that green color," I said.

Well, Dad and I sanded it, and I painted it white. It took

two coats, and now it looks pretty good. I was glad to have that to do. First useful thing I've done this century.

"Want me to paint anything else?" I asked Dad.

He grinned and shook his head. "Not right now, but if I think of anything, I'll ask you."

Then when the paint dried, Dad attempted to hang the door. It turned out that it wasn't a perfect fit after all. Too wide by maybe a quarter of an inch. And too tall, also, is what it looked like to me, by about that same amount.

Dad leaned the door sideways in the doorway and scratched his head.

"What now?" I asked.

"Time to call in the experts," he said. "I know when I'm licked."

So that was how this guy Miles happened to be at the house that day.

Miles was cool. He was a short old guy, wearing a frayed cloth hat and a pair of overalls with a hundred places to put things. He smelled of mint, and he wore a beard that was gray in the center and white for the rest of it.

"Do you care if I watch?" I asked.

"I don't mind the company," he said.

Miles whistled under his breath as he worked. He put the door up. Then he took it down and measured it. Then he sanded it. Put it up again. Then he took it down and measured it again. Sanded. Measured. Sanded. Measured.

"That would drive me crazy," I said. "All the times you put the door up and it's not right yet."

"Well, then it's a good thing I'm the one doing it," Miles answered. His eyes were on his work. "Yup. It's a good thing."

"But doesn't it make you crazy?"

"Nope." He pulled out his measuring tape one more time. "If I felt that way about it, I'd be mad every second. I don't like being mad all that much. Spoils the day." He sanded a small area. "I save being mad for other things."

"Like what?"

"Like—uh—" He paused and looked at me. "I get mad if someone cheats me. But then I don't work with that guy again. I got mad when my father got sick and I couldn't do anything for him. Not that it helped."

"You don't get mad very often," I said.

"What would be the point? Just use your energy to get where you need to get."

"But don't you need to get mad sometimes? Don't things sometimes just make you mad?"

"Sure. I cussed out some guy only last week for trying to sell me the wrong materials. And he fixed my order and gave me a coupon for the next time. You can't roll over and play dead when someone's giving you a raw deal. When my wife left me for another man, I was plenty mad. I'd trusted her, and there she was walking out. I was mad then, no question about that, with steam coming out my ears. But a wife's a little more important than a door."

"What did you do?" I asked.

"When my wife left me? Well, I felt bad for a while. Then one day I took that woman's sewing machine and the fabric and patterns she had in her cabinet and took it all to a homeless shelter. The people there were happy to get it. That helped my mood. I went back the next day with a box of all her favorite foods that she'd left in the pantry. I got to know a few people at the shelter and started helping in the kitchen once in a while too. Met a nice lady one of those times." He winked at me. "She was baking sourdough bread."

"But didn't your wife want the sewing machine?"

"Eventually, but it was long gone by then. I gave her a couple hundred dollars instead." Miles grinned while he measured the door. "She liked that old sewing machine. Now she was going to have to learn how to use a new one. So I pinched her a little bit on that." He picked up the sander, and I watched while he used it. He paused to look over at me to say, "It didn't hurt me one bit."

The next time he put the sander down, I said, "So you don't get mad over doors and stuff? Just people."

"Get mad over a silly piece of wood? The wood's not doing

anything to me. It died when they cut down the tree. I'm the one making the adjustments to this door, not the other way around. I guess I could cuss out myself, but how would that help?"

I laughed. "So you make adjustments."

"That's right. The way I see it, life's a series of small adjustments." He sanded a little more before measuring again.

I thought about that. "Always small?"

"No. But mostly small. Small adjustments all the time that get interrupted by big bangs like wives walking out on you or parents dying. Then it's big fixes before going back to the small adjustments."

"One of my parents died too," I put in. "A year and a half ago. My mom."

He glanced over at me. "I'm sorry." He shook his head. "You're too young for that kind of thing."

"Sometimes I forget that she's dead. Isn't that weird? She died a year and a half ago, and sometimes I still forget." I thought of the orange Popsicles.

"My dad died twenty years ago," Miles said. His eyes were on a far memory. "Sometimes I still want to call him up when the Eagles win. Just for the lightning flash of a moment. Then the next lightning flash moment reminds me that I can't. Boy. We used to go to games together. Take blankets and hot coffee and I'd freeze anyway while Dad yelled and yelled."

Miles put the door up again. Looked like a perfect fit to me. But no. Down it came again.

"That looked just right to me that time," I said.

"You wouldn't have liked it," he said. "It would have stuck." He pointed. "Right there it would have stuck."

Measuring, sanding. Another small adjustment, and Miles swung the door up again. This time it stayed there while he tightened the hinges into place.

Then he put his tools away—the sander, the measuring tape, and a few other things—into the back of his van that seemed to have every tool in the world in it. All orderly and right where you could see it.

He gave me a short nod, and then he started up his van and took it down the road.

I watched him stop at the stop sign at the corner. A total, complete stop, and then an easy right onto Fishers Avenue and he was gone. I heard his van's engine for another minute while he gradually brought it up to speed. *Ererer—errrr—errr!* Then the engine noise faded and flattened until I couldn't pick it out.

I returned to the house and opened the new door. Closed it. Opened it and closed it. It looked good and worked better than the other one ever did.

39.

I told Dad about my conversation with Miles.

"What kind of fixes and small adjustments can you make to survive what Maureen and I survived?" I asked.

"I think you find out when you do them," said Dad. He was chopping celery at the kitchen counter while I wandered about the kitchen, picking up cookbooks and pot holders and stuff and laying them down again.

"Twenty-four dead and two survivors," I said to him. "What can we do?" I opened and closed the flatware drawer.

"More than the dead," he said.

I looked at him. "That's a lousy thing to say."

"There were more than two survivors, Joey," Dad said. "You should look outside yourself."

I didn't know what he meant. My whole class had died

except Maureen and me. There was nobody else. Two survivors. Two.

"I'm a survivor too, Joey," Dad said.

"But you weren't in the school that day."

"Lots of people weren't," he said. "But don't you see it affects me, too? And all those other parents—both whose kids died and whose didn't. Plus those teachers and all the kids who did get out of the building. They're survivors too. We're survivors because we're still here."

"I know, Dad," I said, "but Maureen and I. We were part of the class that died. We were supposed to die too."

"Who says so?"

"That's what people think. If we didn't die, we must have set the fire."

"That's a kind of convoluted logic," said Dad.

"But that's how people think." Like in *Hamlet*. I saw now that that's what Ruby-ruby meant. If Maureen and I didn't die, we must have set the fire. Claudius was the murderer because he got the girl, and Maureen and I were murderers because we got to live. Huh!

Dad was talking. "Maybe Mr. Austen set the fire," he said. "Have you thought of that?"

I gave Dad a double take. "*Mr. Austen!* He was trying to teach. He was *determined* to teach that day."

"Maybe he was also trying to kill a classroom full of kids."

160

"Dad!"

"I'm just trying to show you, Joey. There's more than one way to look at this. Maybe nobody set the fire. Maybe fifteen people from Greenland did. Who can know? But one thing I do know—you were not supposed to be one of the victims. Stop talking like that."

"Well, it feels that way."

"I don't care. You're here and you're my son. My son was not supposed to die. Nobody was *supposed* to die. There's no nothin' about *supposed to* involved in any of this. But just suppose there was. I still say it. You weren't supposed to be one of the victims. Ask me why not."

"Why not?"

"Because you're here. And you're here because you knew. You knew the danger."

"They were all people who knew that," I said. "They weren't two-year-olds. They'd seen fire before."

"They knew, but not the way you did," Dad said.

I stared at the snapshot my brain wouldn't let go of and shook my head. "But, Dad, now I've lost all those people. Mom and—and all those kids. It's hard to get used to it."

"Of course it is."

"Even Mr. Austen. And I didn't even like him."

"Foolish man."

"Yeah. But that didn't mean he should die."

"I know. But it's why he died."

I was quiet. I didn't know what to say.

"Look, Joey, Miles was right about a lot when he was talking about adjustments. But there's more to it than that."

"Like what?"

"Think of life as a long car ride," Dad said.

"A car ride."

"A journey. It is a journey. It's not about destinations, really. It's about the journey. The car ride. What we do along the way."

"All right. We're all on car rides."

"And, besides luck, what gets you a good long car ride is your ability to be a driving ace. To think on your feet, to do what's right."

"You mean how well you avoid problems?"

"Not just that. It's how you deal with them and think your way through them when they hit you in the face. And how well you stay true to yourself. That's what you did. That's why you're here. You stayed true to yourself."

"But what about those other kids? Weren't they true to themselves?"

"Maybe. Probably. They just didn't come from your experience. Being true to yourself doesn't necessarily mean a tree won't fall on you. That's where luck comes into it."

"Luck! Some luck to lose your mother!"

"Luck doesn't have to be good, Joey. It's just luck. The way the cards fall. Your mother died because of a fire. Luck. And you learned from that. Luck."

"Who couldn't learn from that?"

"Still—luck. And, in spite of your question, not everybody learns the obvious lesson from experience. But you did. Your mom died because of a fire and you learned from it. Call it luck or whatever you want. It saved your life."

I sighed again. "So we're back to that."

"Yes." Dad chopped real hard and celery danced away from the knife and onto the floor. "You got yourself outside that day at school because you knew." He squatted to pick up the celery from the floor and tossed it into the garbage. "You *knew*!"

"But that means that Mom had to die if I was going to live. I don't want it to be that way."

"She didn't die so you could live. She just died. Saving you from the school fire had nothing to do with it. If it had been about the school fire, what do you think she would have done?"

"You mean if she'd known about it in advance?"

"Yes."

"Well, first, she'd have kept me home. Assuming she was still alive."

"Right. And what else?"

I thought of how Mom would have objected to Mr. Austen saying "hell" and "damn" in the classroom. How she would have spoken up, made herself unpopular . . . kind of . . . like . . . me. . . .

"She would have—" I hesitated.

"Yes?" Dad made an encouraging gesture with a spatula.

"She would have done her best to keep *everybody* out of that building. Not just me. Nobody would have died if she'd had anything to say about it."

"There you go," said Dad. "Now you're cooking with gas."

He put the celery into a bowl with ground beef and broke an egg over it.

I sat down at the kitchen table. "Hm." I said. "Hm."

"Well said," said Dad. "I couldn't have put it better myself."

40.

I was outside on the porch listening to the Atterberg and petting Preston when Dad came out.

"Telephone," he said. He held out the cordless.

Who would call?

"Who is it?"

"Derek Masterman. He says he knows you from school."

Derek Masterman?

I turned down the volume on the boom box and took the phone. "Hello."

Derek Masterman? Why was he calling me?

"Hey, dude," I heard.

"Hi." I wasn't going out on any limb.

"How are you?"

"Fine. What do you want?" I took the notebook and rolled it into a small telescope.

"Hey, I'm the guy who wouldn't let Mr. Pavarotti's class kill you, remember?"

"I remember. And I thank you. Is that why you called?"

"No. Just trying to make sure you knew who I was."

The biggest guy in the school thought he was anonymous? "I knew who you were before. The star athlete." Rolling and rolling the notebook to a smaller and smaller tube.

Derek laughed. "On this square quarter mile."

"Well, what is it?" I flattened the telescope and stuck it inside my belt. I clipped a Holiday Inn pen onto the telescope. "Why did you call?"

"My parents run a frame shop."

"My dad's a computer engineer. Good-bye."

"Wait. My parents run the frame shop that's framing your picture."

"What picture? You mean my *sketch*?" Suddenly the air around me was red with black specks.

"Yeah. That's a great picture."

I wanted to thrust my arm through the red-aired miles to the frame shop and grab that sketch back so fast—

"Did you really draw it?"

"Of course I really drew it. Do you think my dad takes other kids' artwork to be framed?"

"Don't be so prickly. I just wanted to let you know I saw it. It's great."

"Thanks." I didn't have anything else to say. Except *Stop looking at my sketch!* I blinked at the beech tree to keep the red away. Green. Green. Green and brown. Blink.

"Peter Vitti's father saw it too. I thought you might like to know."

"Pete's dad saw it?" Blink.

"And Priscilla Ramirez—her mother's been in to see it." Blink, blink.

"What?" I cupped my hand over the receiver. "Dad! Dad!" I was starting to sweat and my heart was racing. "Dad!"

Dad came out of the kitchen, a frying pan in his hand. "What? What's wrong?"

Derek was still talking. Donnie's parents, Michelle's parents, Simone's grandmother and aunt . . .

I handed Dad the receiver to get away from the names. Then I ran. I ran for the bathroom, where I banged my fists against the wall. I banged and banged and banged against that hard tile.

So half the world had seen that sketch. It was out in the open.

Dad left right away to get it, to get it away from everybody's eyes. But it was too late. They'd seen it.

I didn't know what to do.

That sketch showed everything. It was personal, like the journal. Now everybody could see what room E201 looked like that day. Through my eyes.

NO!

41.

August 4th

My sketch. It's an extension of my brain, a piece I didn't mean to share with anybody except maybe Dad.

I drew everybody the way they looked the last time I saw them alive. I drew them plus the pink elephant and the easel and the portrait of Robert E. Lee hanging on the wall way in the back of the room. I drew all of that because I had to.

Donnie and Jamaal and Cheryl and Pete and Myrna and Priscilla and

Priscilla.

She wore Deely Boppers in her hair a lot the year before last. All day long, bouncing those sparkly green Deely Boppers. I wanted to grab them off her head and throw them out the window. *Stop acting like that!* That's what I wanted to shout at her. *Stop acting like that and sit still!* But she always acted like that whether you shouted at her or not. All bouncy and a pain.

She was a pain with those Deely Boppers. They made me mad, the way they moved. But maybe that was because— I don't know why. This year she'd spiked her hair in every direction with purple on the ends. Maybe next year she would have gone to braids with ribbons wound through them, or maybe she would have cut off all her hair and tattooed her forehead with hearts. You never knew with Priscilla. She might do anything.

She always said she wanted to be a Spanish teacher. She could already speak Spanish because that's what they speak in her house. But would she have been a teacher? Would she have been a Deely-Bopping Spanish teacher with purple spiked hair? I'll never know.

So I put the purple in her hair when I drew the picture. That would help me remember what kind of girl she was. Same thing with Donnie's cowlick and Myrna's hand under her chin while she slouched the way tall people slouch, and Pete's scar and the way his jaw stuck out that day.

I was there when Pete got that scar. He was clowning around on the deck of the pool in his backyard. We were all laughing, and I could hardly stand up, I was laughing so hard. Just the way he was talking. Laughing and walking across the diving board like he was walking the plank on Captain Hook's ship. Laughing and laughing and pretending he was going to jump in and then not jumping in, just clowning around.

Laughing and laughing, all of us, and then—he fell in.

At first I thought he'd meant to, but then I heard the crack of his head on the board. Blood trailed in the water over him as he went down, and Mr. Vitti was in there so fast, pulling Peter out onto the deck. He was all right, and as soon as he stopped choking, he was back laughing.

"Pretty good joke, huh, Ma?" he asked while his mother tried to stop the bleeding.

"Oh, Peter," she said. But she couldn't keep from smiling either, even though the rest of her face showed she was upset.

Nine stitches he got for that. Laugh lines he calls the scars. Called. But when I think of him laughing, I can't believe he's dead. Someone who laughed like that?

So when I drew the sketch, I have him the way I last saw him, sure, with his chin kind of sticking out like he was mad, but I also did a second face, kind of a ghost face next to the first. The ghost face shows him laughing like he did the day he got the scar.

After I drew that ghost face, I put in others—Priscilla wearing her Deely Boppers, Simone playing her flute with her hair hanging over her fingers. How did it not get tangled up in the keys? Donnie bouncing a soccer ball off his head, Myrna with that thinking-hard look of hers you'd see when she was talking math to Mr. Miller. Because those were the things that showed who they were when they weren't scared or worried, just doing their ordinary things. Those things I worked in with that last snapshot my brain took.

When I was finished, I went back and put wings on everyone's shoulders.

Even Mr. Austen's.

42.

August 6th

That tree planting ceremony.

They want me to come. The Vittis and Simone's family and Priscilla's and all of them. All because of my sketch. They want me to come and talk about the sketch and why I drew what I drew.

That picture. I bled to draw it. Those pencil lines are my blood that flowed from my veins. I didn't draw it to be smart or funny or creative or because I was bored or anything like that. I had to record that moment. It was important, maybe the most important thing I've ever done. That drawing shows all there is to show the moment that everything changed.

Well, I don't know. What's to keep someone from wanting to shoot me or something? But Dad says anybody that ever saw my sketch would know I couldn't have started any fire. That picture says it all.

43.

"Hey! Hey, Joey!"

I looked toward the street from my usual spot on the porch steps. Derek Masterman and an older version of him were standing at the gate.

I unlocked it and gestured for them to come in before locking it again.

"This is my dad," said Derek. "He needs a break from my driving. We saw you on your porch, so we stopped."

Mr. Masterman laughed. "Derek's getting the idea of the gearshift," he told me.

"I only stalled four times," said Derek.

"You've got your permit?" I asked. "That's pretty cool, but I thought you'd have your license by now."

Derek glanced at his father. "Dad didn't think I was mature enough to drive when I was sixteen."

Susan Shaw

Mr. Masterman rolled his eyes skyward, but he didn't say anything.

"I know, Dad," said Derek. "You're not so sure now, but I'll do better on the way home." He looked at me. "We thought I should have my license before I went off to college, at least."

Dad came out through the sliding glass door. "Company?" he asked. "I heard voices."

I introduced Dad to the Mastermans.

"Nice to meet you," said Dad. He shook Mr. Masterman's hand, and then Derek's. "Anyone like some coffee? I just brewed some high-test."

"After experiencing the dark side of driving lessons," said Mr. Masterman, "I could use a cup of high-test."

"Oh, really?" Dad opened the door and gestured for Mr. Masterman to go in ahead of him. "Derek's a new driver?"

"The word 'driver' might be a stretch," answered Mr. Masterman.

The door closed behind them, and I was left on the porch with Derek. What was I supposed to do with him?

"You didn't just happen by, did you?" I asked.

"No, we came on purpose, but Dad was very happy to get out of the car, anyway." He rolled his eyes at me and shook his head. "I almost didn't see the stop sign at the foot of the hill, and when I did, I slammed on the brakes. My dear papa

174

was not pleased." He said "papa" with the accent on the second syllable. Pa*pa*. "We stalled. Then I flooded the engine, so we pushed the car to the curb and walked the last half a block."

"Uh-huh. So you're here. What do you want?"

"I thought I'd check on you."

"Oh." What was that supposed to mean? Check on me?

"So how are you?" Derek asked.

"I'm fine," I said.

"Sure you are," he said. "Sitting in your backyard all summer."

"How do you know that?"

"It's what people say. Hey, look at your cat!" He bent down to pet Preston, but I stood in his way.

"Preston's pretty fragile," I said. "He's old."

"We have a fifteen-year-old cat," Derek said. "Mehitabel. We call her Mellie."

"Preston's twenty. He was my mother's cat when she was a kid."

"No kidding. Wow. You don't mind if I pet him, do you? I'll be careful."

I let him pass, and he lowered his huge frame next to Preston on the sleeping bag and petted him. I didn't like it because I didn't know Derek, but he was the one who saved me that day in Mr. Pavarotti's room, so I didn't say anything, just watched, making sure.

Preston lifted his head and stared at Derek with his green eyes. He purred. Preston thought Derek was all right, anyway.

"How're ya doin', old guy?" Derek asked him. He stroked under Preston's chin. Preston raised his neck to push against Derek's fingers. "How are ya doin'?"

"So you're an animal person?" I asked. I sat cross-legged on the floor a few feet away.

"Sure am. I want to be a veterinarian."

I watched Derek pet Preston for another minute. Then I asked him again. "What brings you here? Really."

"Just checking on you. Really."

"Why?"

"Why?" he repeated.

"Yeah, why? You don't know me or anything."

"I've been thinking about you ever since the fire, especially since I grabbed you from the jaws of death."

I laughed at "jaws of death." "What happened to you when you went back in the room?" I asked.

Then we heard it.

"Murderers! Murderers!"

Derek stopped petting Preston and looked up. "What's that?"

I didn't answer. That lady with the flowery hat was back.

Crash! Garbage and broken glass hit the driveway.

"Murderers! Murderers!"

Dad and Mr. Masterman came out in a rush.

"What's going on?" asked Derek's dad.

Derek leaned over the edge of the porch so he could see better. "Well, will you look at that." Red-faced, I picked up the dustpan and brush. I wished Derek and his dad hadn't been around to see this.

Derek unfolded his great size and started for the gate. Unfolded. Now I understood what Shakespeare meant. The watchman must have been tall. I was startled into thinking that Derek was my watchman. Unfolding his tallness to guard. Huh!

"Murderers!"

"Stay here," said Mr. Masterman to his son. He looked at Dad. "Do you mind if I handle this?"

"Go right ahead," said Dad.

Crash! Another load of trash hit the driveway. "Murderers!"

"Ms. Austen!" Mr. Masterman jogged to the gate. "What the heck!"

"Oh! Mr. Masterman! I didn't see you. And is that Derek? What are you doing here?"

"Visiting friends. What are *you* doing here?"

She didn't answer right away. *Wait,* I thought, *Ms. Austen? Ms. Austen?*

Susan Shaw

"Well, somebody has to do something," she said. "They're not even going to arrest these kids. And why are the Campbells your friends? Joseph Campbell is a murderer!"

"Ms. Austen," said Derek's dad, "go home." He looked at the trash dumped on the driveway between him and the gate. "I should make you clean up this mess and call the police."

"It's his fault. How did he know? Answer me that. How did he know it was a real fire if he didn't set it? My father died. The kid would have told him the truth about the fire if he was innocent. How did he know?"

Mr. Masterson turned to me, me standing there with the dustpan and brush in my hands. I knew my mouth hung open big enough to catch a robin. Ms. *Austen*?

"Tell her, Joey," he said. "Tell the lady how you knew to get out."

I moved my eyes from Ms. Austen and stared at *him*. "What do you mean?"

"Just tell her why you left your history class that day."

"Because the alarm was going off."

"Liar," said the lady—Ms. Austen.

"Wait," I said to Derek. Dad and Derek had inched forward onto the driveway with me. "Is this Mr. Austen's daughter?"

"Yeah. She's pretty mad at you."

"Mad!" she yelled. "You killed my father. *Mad*. That's nowhere near it."

"She's out of her mind," Dad said. "She needs someone to blame."

"But it was her father who wouldn't leave," I said. "He's the one who wouldn't let anybody go. He gave me a detention for walking out. Maureen, too."

Everybody stopped to stare at me then, even Dad. I guessed I hadn't told him that part.

"A detention?" Dad asked. Then he looked at Ms. Austen. "A detention? A detention? Did you hear that, Ms. Austen?"

"My father would never have done that. He was a good man."

"Your father wanted us to know about the Spanish-American War," I said. "He cared a lot about that." I didn't add that he cared more about that than saving our lives. I didn't add that he yelled so much he scared everybody else into staying put. "That's what he cared about," I repeated more softly.

Ms. Austen looked at her feet. "That was his passion." Her voice was toneless.

So then I knew she didn't think I was the killer anymore.

"Go home, Ms. Austen," said Mr. Masterman. "Don't come back."

We watched her walk, head down, back to her blue and white hatchback. We watched her start up the car. We watched her leave.

Derek grabbed the dustpan and brush from me and set to

work on the mess while the rest of us returned to the porch.

"You okay?" Dad asked me.

"Sure," I said. I felt a little spacey, but I was all right. Ms. *Austen*? Mr. Austen's *daughter*?

Dad and Mr. Masterman went back to the kitchen for the rest of their coffee.

"How do you know that lady?" I asked Derek.

"She was my English teacher last year." Derek dumped a load into the trash can, and I walked back with him when he went back for more. "Didn't you recognize her?"

"I didn't know Mr. Austen's daughter taught at our school."

"Sure. She teaches Spanish, too. But she's actually not Ms. Austen anymore. Mrs. Cantelmo. That's her name now. She got married."

He finished with the cleanup, and we wandered back to the porch. We sat there for a while and talked. About the weather, about baseball, about cats.

It was good to talk with a friend.

44.

Maureen and I went to the tree planting ceremony.
I stayed in the back, off to the side most of the time, standing behind Dad near an exit. Just in case. Just in case things got weird.

Ruby-ruby and Albert were there too, sitting in the seats nearest us. I was glad they came. People on my side.

Maureen sat with her mother in the last row. She wore a veil that was blue but so dark that it was just short of black. The veil covered her eyes and half of her nose. If you didn't know it was Maureen under there, you couldn't have recognized her—she was so thin now, and her hair— Well, she'd cut off all the black hair, so what was left was blond and real short. And that veil—it was so thick, I don't know how she could see through it.

Twenty-four saplings lined the front of the room—a sapling

for each person who'd died. Different kinds of saplings, depending on what the families wanted. Oaks, maples, pines. All kinds. One was a holly tree. Taking turns with a wireless mike, one person spoke next to the different trees while another held up a picture of the person the tree was going to represent.

Most of the people spoke so softly that I could barely hear them, but I guess that didn't matter. Words couldn't really say what they felt. Plus, I didn't listen. I tried, but then my eyes would shift and I'd be looking through the crowd, almost seeing those missing people.

Ms. Austen spoke. Well, Mrs. Cantelmo. Without the hat, I kind of recognized her from school. She looked like Mr. Austen, sort of, with the same blond hair that faded into brown toward the back of her head. Maybe she knew the story of the crazed principal who had run one fire drill after another until they took him away. She didn't say.

"My father loved teaching," is what she said. She held the mike in her left hand while a man, probably Mr. Cantelmo, held her right hand in one of his while holding Mr. Austen's portrait with the other. "He loved working with high school kids and teaching them the lessons we can learn from American history."

Did he? Maybe. It was hard to tell. But on the day of the fire, something was important to him about making sure we knew about the *Maine*. Maybe he wanted us to beware of mass hysteria. *Don't worry about that,* I'd like to say to him. *I got that lesson down pat.*

I glanced around the room at my missing classmates— that sounds funny, but that's what I did. I glanced around to where they should have been and let out a quiet breath.

Dad touched me on the shoulder. "You okay?"

I nodded.

"You don't have to do this," he said. "We can leave any- time. I'll just tell the chairman as we go."

"That's okay," I said. "I want to."

Because it was the last thing Maureen and I could do for our friends who had died. And they were all our friends, mine at least, even Mr. Austen, even though maybe I didn't get that until later. Not all friends in the usual sense but people that held my world together. People I cared about even if I didn't always know it.

Someone removed the sheet that covered my framed drawing where it sat on an easel. Actually, a copy of it. I was still afraid something would happen to it if just anyone could get near it.

The original was on the wall of my bedroom in the frame Dad had picked out. I didn't know if I wanted it to stay there, but it was there for the time being. At least until I moved back inside with the cold weather. If I did. I wasn't sure about that yet. And I wasn't sure I wanted it where I could see it all the time. But Dad said we could move it or put a curtain over it if we wanted. Later.

When the sheet came down, it was our turn—Maureen's and mine. Heads turned and whispers began while Dad walked me to the front where the podium was. Maureen came up the aisle with her mother. I could tell people still didn't recognize her.

When I got to the front, I looked around at the people before me. I didn't know most of them. Little glimpses of the fire victims showed in some of the faces, so I could tell whose family was whose.

Donnie's older brother had that same cowlick. Their father was bald. Maybe that's how you lose the cowlick. Except for a sprinkling of gray, Priscilla's mom had the same coal black hair as Priscilla, but no purple. I looked for Priscilla's ready grin in her mother's face. Naturally, it wasn't there. Not on a day like that. But I could see lines that might crease into it.

The audience waited while Maureen and I stood before them, Maureen flanked by her mother. Dad stood tense, right up close to me, touching me with his arm. I knew at the first sign of anything funny, Dad's body would be shielding mine. Maureen's mom seemed poised too, searching the faces in the crowd before us for anything that might go wrong.

I looked at Maureen. I was close enough to see her raise her eyebrows at me through the veil.

"Hello," she spoke into the microphone.

That's when people got it. I heard her name murmured up and down the rows.

"Yes," she said. She raised her veil. "I'm Maureen McGillicuddy, and I'm standing next to Joey Campbell. You know us. We're the survivors from room E201. Mr. and Mrs. Vitti asked us to speak today because we were the last people to see Mr. Austen and the rest of our unfortunate history class." Maureen turned her face away from the microphone and let out a loud breath. She turned back, took in some air, and started again. "Well, I'm not much of a speaker, and I'm going to let Joey do that part, but I do write poetry. I'd like to share this poem with you."

A wave of sound rolled across the crowd. You could tell that the audience was on the fence about letting her continue. Then Maureen plunged in with her poem, and it didn't take the crowd long to get quiet.

I'm only fifteen, the young girl said
So much time to move ahead
I want to be a high school teacher
Or maybe a clown or a new age preacher

I want to fly up to a cloud
I want to make my parents proud

Susan Shaw

I want to have a million babies
I want to clear the world of rabies

I'm going to the senior prom
I'll go with Mike or maybe Tom
I'll wear pink or maybe blue
But that's still in a year or two

I'm fifteen, there's so much time
I change my mind each day in rhyme
I climb a tree 'cause I'm kid
And kids climb trees, they always did

When I grow up—I'll still climb trees
I'll study bark and honeybees
I'll parachute through waves of mist
I'll have that first romantic kiss

My life will be a wondrous thing
You'll see—my joy will make you sing
But I'm fifteen—I've lots of time
To change my mind each day in rhyme

I'm only fifteen, the young girl said
So much time to move ahead

One of the Survivors

I want to be a high school teacher
Or maybe a clown or a new age preacher

Maureen choked on the last couple of words. I found myself choking too. It looked to me like everybody was having trouble with tears.

Maureen turned to her mother, and for a few moments they hugged each other. I waited, partly because I wasn't ready to talk and partly because I wasn't sure Maureen was finished. Eventually her mother released her, and she turned back to the microphone.

"I dedicate that poem to my missing friends, knowing the unfairness of my chances when they have lost theirs. And I want to say one more thing." Maureen looked down, and I could hear her long breath and the exhalation. Then she looked directly out at all the survivors before us. "Good-bye, my lost friends. I love you all."

Then she and her mother returned through the aisle toward their seats.

Dad started the applause, and then a couple of people in the front row began. Then it was everywhere. Maureen and her mother paused most of the way back. Maureen nodded through the clapping—once, and then again—before taking her seat in the back row. Her mother took her place by her side, and while I watched, Maureen once more pulled the veil of deep blue over her face.

Then the room became quiet and it was my turn.

My hands were sweating, and all I wanted to do was race away from there to anywhere else. But I stayed where I was and opened my folder on the lectern. I had a bunch of notes in there, and my journal, too, but I still didn't know what I was going to say.

I looked out at the faces all turned toward me. I looked at Dad at my side, down at the folder.

"Hello," I said, and my voice was so loud with the mike. "Hello." I spoke softer, wondering if I'd get past that first word. What was I going to say to these people?

I glanced down at my journal. It was actually three notebooks held together with a rubber band. Three notebooks, all with red covers, three notebooks all with Mr. Trama's picture because I'd copied the first one into the other two. But three notebooks! Who knew I would write so many words, so many sentences, draw so many pictures, that I'd need three notebooks?

"Hello," I said again. "My name is Joseph Edward Campbell." I lifted my rubber-banded journal and waved it in the air. "This is my journal." I felt the audience tense. Why? Were they afraid of what was in it? Maybe. "I started it in response to the school fire that took away so many of our friends." Pause. What else could I do? Say?

The people before me were silent while I took off the rubber band, and when I looked at them, their eyes were all on me.

I read some of the places where I'd written about sketching the picture. Why I drew the different faces, the ones the last moment of that fateful day in May and the other ones, the ones that showed who those kids were. I talked about Priscilla's Deely Boppers and that they had driven me crazy, and how Pete had gotten his laugh lines, and how I couldn't figure out how Simone had been able to play the flute with all that hair hanging over the keys. How Donnie could bounce a soccer ball over and over on his head without getting a headache.

Then I put the journal aside.

"This—" I pointed to the framed copy. "This is the picture I wrote about. The only two people missing from it are Maureen and me, because Maureen was already out of the room, and you're looking through my eyes. There is one addition. My mother."

A slight buzz met that remark.

I looked at the picture, the place where Mom was sitting cross-legged on the back table, eating an orange Popsicle. Her mouth was curved and she had that we've-got-a-secret look on her face. Good ol' Mom.

"I drew until I felt finished, and when I was finished, my

mom was sitting in the back, watching it all. And Mom, she's the reason I left the room when Mr. Austen told us not to. It was her voice inside my head that made me go. She's the reason Maureen left too, because Maureen knew I wouldn't ever fool around like that—stand up to a teacher and walk out. But that's what happened. And that's the reason everyone else stayed. Because Mr. Austen said to. They obeyed, and Maureen and I didn't."

I let my eyes sweep the room, pausing on Mrs. Cantelmo. Her head was bent. It had to be hard for her to hear what I was saying, but it seemed important to say it.

"Maureen knew me better than anybody else in the room, and that's the reason she's the one who came with me. I really wish more of them had known me that well. If there is one thing I have wished for over and over again, it is that they had all known me that well."

I took in a deep breath.

"I didn't draw this picture to share, any more than I kept a journal to share. I drew it because I had to. I had to bring outside of me what I kept seeing over and over again. That last second before I left the room. It just felt so important."

Then I stopped talking. I couldn't think of another thing to say. Then I could.

"Like you," I said, "Maureen and I will never be the same again. But we will move on, and no matter how long we live—whether it's one more year or a hundred—we will do good things with our lives, at least partly because we knew the people who died in room E201. And we owe to them the effort to make the best that we can of our lives. Because we can."

45.

It was over.

People came up to me after the memorial service and shook my hand. They told me how sorry they were that I'd lost so many friends. They told me they didn't hold me responsible.

"After all," said Mr. Vitti, "the whole rest of the school got outside. Mr. Austen had time to get his class outside too, if you and Maureen made it."

Finally. Somebody said out loud what they had to have known all along. Maureen and I didn't keep Mr. Austen's class from escaping.

"Wonderful speech," said Mr. Bednarik. "Wonderful." He shook my hand and clapped me on the shoulder before disappearing into the crowd.

Erik Wiley, the kid at the car wash on Lancaster Avenue, came up to Dad and me in the parking lot. He was looking taller and his shoulders were wider than when he'd lived down the street.

"Remember me?" he asked.

"Sure I remember you," I said. "How are you?" I shook his hand, and then Dad shook it. We introduced Erik to Ruby-ruby and Albert, who stayed right close to me like they were still afraid something bad might happen.

"I haven't seen you at the car wash lately," said Dad. "How's it going?"

"I'm still working there," Erik told us, "but I'm going to college, too. I'm not a dropout anymore."

"That's great." I looked beyond him at Maureen. She was talking to Gary Chaplin.

Derek Masterman and his dad neared us. "Gotta go pack for college," Derek said as they continued on by, "but I'll call you." *Good,* I thought, nodding. A good friend.

"Where?" Dad asked Erik. "Where are you going?"

I looked again at Maureen and Gary. For once Gary wasn't teasing her and she wasn't getting ready to toss him into his locker. A serious conversation, it looked like to me.

"Montco," said Erik. "The community college. I'm getting my high school diploma and starting on my bachelor's at the same time. Maybe I'll finish at Temple."

"That's really great," I said. "Congratulations."

Susan Shaw

"Terrific," said Dad.

Erik left then. "Have to get to work," he said over his shoulder. "Work, school—that's what I do."

We waved good-bye to him, and then I looked up at Dad.

"It looks like Erik's not going to have to work in a car wash forever," he said. "That's great news."

"You don't have to stay a dropout," I said.

"It's probably a good idea not to start as one," he answered.

Dad, Ruby-ruby, Albert, me, Maureen, and Maureen's mom went to our house for dinner after that. Ruby-ruby and Albert cooked. Barbecued chicken and rice and green beans. Vanilla ice cream and raspberry ripple frozen yogurt for dessert.

46.

The day after the ceremony Maureen and I filled in the hole I'd dug in the backyard. That was one big hole and we worked at it for a while.

"You know," said Maureen at one point. She rested her shovel on the ground and gazed at me. "People who want to go to China from here usually take airplanes. Some take ships. But they never dig."

The point of my shovel was tipped into the pile. "Oh, yeah?" I returned. I flipped the tipful of dirt at her.

"Yeah!" She tossed some at me. Then I tossed more at her. Pretty soon, dirt was flying everywhere but into the hole. Toss, toss, toss! Dirt and dust filled the air like a brown fog. Toss, toss, toss! The brown fog covered us both with its fine touch.

"Heeeeey!" That was Dad from the porch.

Maureen and I stopped instantly and looked at him. His arms were on his hips, and he was shaking his head. Maureen's eyes turned toward mine. Mine turned toward hers. She kept a straight face, but I heard some held-in laughter. *Kh-kh-kh-kh!* I bit my cheek to keep mine quiet.

"You think you're seven years old?" Dad asked. *Swat!* "No more of that stuff! If you can't behave"—*swat!*—"Maureen will have to go home!" He turned back to the house. "Sheesh!" *Swat!* He escaped again through the sliding glass door.

Maureen and I looked at each other and started to laugh. We returned to the pile with our shovels and went back to filling in the hole. Laughing.

It felt good. I was glad I'd dug that hole. Because with each shovelful I put back, I felt a little better. That's when I noticed. That crater, that hole I'd lived in for months, was gone.

Well, not completely. I still had that hole. It had two parts. One of them had my history class in it—all those people who'd died. The other had Mom in it. But the hole didn't come out of my heart and surround me anymore like an underground roofless cavern. It had retreated to just my heart, and I could live with that.

When we finished, Maureen put down her shovel.

"This is the end," she said. "Don't you feel it?"

I put my shovel down too. "I do."

"Should we do something?" asked Maureen.

"Like recite a poem?"

"No more poems," said Maureen. "Not for this."

"I had been thinking of burying my journal in this hole," I said. "I put the ashes from one entry in there already."

"Which entry?" asked Maureen.

"The one about the parking lot after the fire. With the firefighters bringing out the bodies."

"It's too bad you burned that," she said. "That was the most important part of the whole story."

"I could write it again," I said. "Maybe not in quite the same way."

"Do that," she urged. "Do that and keep the whole thing together."

"But why?"

"Because it's a record. It tells the truth of something important that happened that people may want to know later. Don't bury the truth."

I thought about that. "You're right," I said.

"Of course I'm right," said Maureen with a grin, "but I think you're right too that we should put something into the hole. Something that belongs to just us."

"What belongs to us?" Then I thought of something. "Wait." I ran into the house and came back with a pair of scissors. I gave them to Maureen. "Cut off some of my hair."

She looked at me doubtfully. "You want me to cut your hair?"

"Just a little. Then I'm going to cut a little piece of yours."

She ran fingers through her short hair. "It can only be a little piece."

Then she cut a tuft of hair from the back of my head. I took the scissors and cut some from hers. I touched the area afterward.

"I don't think you can see what's missing," I said.

"It doesn't matter if you can," said Maureen. "It'll grow back."

I showed her the blond strands in my palm. "Put mine with it," I said, and she did. I mixed them around so you could see blond and black together. "So it's one thing," I explained. "From us to them."

"I understand."

Then I gave the hair to her to hold while I dug out some of the dirt. Maybe four shovelfuls because I didn't want the hair to find its way to the surface. Then Maureen placed the black and blond hair at the bottom of the new hole. She stroked it. I knelt next to her and did the same thing. Then we pushed the dirt back over it.

We stood up and walked away from the filled-in hole. Maureen smiled at me, and I smiled at her. I felt the best that I had in a long time.

"Dad said I could finish high school at Montco like Erik Wiley," I told her. "Do you want to do that?"

"No," she said. "I'm going back to Village Park High School."

"Aren't you afraid?" I asked.

She looked at me with those blue eyes that know what's true. "Sure," she said with an impish grin, "but no one's going to keep me out, and that's a fack, Jack."

So—I decided to go back with her.

Here is your first glimpse of

Tunnel Vision

by Susan Shaw

A couple of days later we got the call from Mr. Treves that our box had been delivered from Kansas.

"Let's go." Dad handed me my sunglasses and hat. He was wearing the glasses from Mr. Treves.

"Movie-star mode?" I asked.

"Movie-star mode," he answered. He hit the garage door opener, and we went through to the garage, where Dad handed me the van keys.

"My turn?" I asked.

"I kind of like being chauffeured around by my daughter. Turns the tables on you just a little bit."

"Ha!"

After a time Dad directed me onto a ramp of the interstate. I'd driven on interstates before, but this one had concrete Jersey barriers that took away the shoulders and narrowed the lanes.

"I don't like this." I gritted my teeth.

"Take a deep breath," Dad said. "You're doing fine."

I took a bunch of deep breaths, and I did okay, just didn't love it. Fortunately there wasn't much traffic, but I was sure going to be glad when we got past the barriers. When would they end?

"I wonder why they call them Jersey barriers," I said.

"I don't know," said Dad. "Maybe—"

A purple car shot around us at high speed, then cut in front of the van. I jammed on the brakes so I wouldn't hit it and screeched toward the passing lane, the only place to go. The driver of the other car shot forward again and disappeared around a curve.

"Man!" I was out of breath.

"What an imbecile! You all right?"

Before I could answer, another car, a blue one, came up behind us, tailgating and honking before also swerving around me. And then there was the purple car again, waiting on a temporary pull-off before it came up honking behind the van. The honking car, I saw in the rearview mirror, had a couple of people in the front seat. They were laughing. Laughing hard.

The car got closer to my bumper, closer and closer. *Honk-honk-honk-honk-honk-BANG!* The van lurched under us. The occupants of the purple car laughed harder on the impact.

BANG! Again. Again they roared. It was the funniest thing in the world to them.

I tried to pass the blue car to get away, but it moved as I moved and stayed on the line between the lanes. I was trapped.

"He's going to hit us again," said Dad.

BANG!

An exit coming up. Could we last that long? *BANG!* And again. *BANG!* We got to the small opening, and I peeled off as the car behind us—*BANG!*—hit us again. Too fast, too fast. I struggled for control.

Dad's head faced the rear. "They couldn't react fast enough to follow us. Good job!"

Finally I could slow down. Then I pulled over onto the shoulder and stopped. I let out a deep breath, then another. I took my fingers off the steering wheel and put them over my face, through my hair. Another deep breath.

"That was close," said Dad. He closed his eyes.

Deep breath, deep breath. "Was that the Core, do you think?" Deep breath.

"I wouldn't doubt it."

"We could have died."

"I don't think they cared."